Infinity

Cameron Hart

Published by Cameron Hart, 2024.

INFINITY

First edition. July 1, 2024.

Copyright © 2024 Cameron Hart.

ISBN: 979-8227948151

Written by Cameron Hart.

Want a free book?

Sign up for my newsletter[1] and get your free copy of Chasing Stacy!

One look at the stunning waitress carrying the weight of the world on her shoulders, and I'm a goner. I wasn't looking for a sweet little thing with auburn hair and more baggage than I can fit on the back of my bike, but there's no going back now. She's mine. I'll prove to her I'm more than capable of handling her past and making her feel safe again.

---

1. https://dl.bookfunnel.com/7wbqvhsx8r

Chapter One

Hudson

"Make sure to order lots of Bulleit bourbon for Jack Montgomery. He likes his drink like he likes his women. Expensive."

I choke on the water I was sipping, nearly spitting it out all over the bar top. "Grams!" I laugh.

"What? It's the worst kept secret in town that old man Jack has paid for company on occasion."

"Does he like his women from Kentucky, too?"

"What? Why would you say a silly thing like that?" Grams asks incredulously.

"Bulleit bourbon. It's from a distillery in Kentucky."

"You know I don't care about details like that," she scoffs, waving her hand in the air dismissively.

"Only when they pertain to the residents of Rosewood, then," I mutter. Grams gives me a sharp look before breaking out into her signature sassy smile. I chuckle and shake my head.

Grams, aka Connie Wolf, is the worst gossip in town. The feisty eighty-eight-year-old likes to think of herself as the town curator. By that, she means she curates the best and latest gossip. She's not mean-spirited, though. If Grams ever hears of someone in need, she pulls strings behind the scenes to make sure everyone is taken care of. This town is her family as much as I am.

"Any other requests?" I ask, checking the list of alcohol before placing the order with my suppliers.

"As long as you have everything to make my favorite drink, I'm good."

"What's your favorite drink? I don't think I've made you anything since I officially took over last month."

"Sex on the beach."

This time, I do spit out my water. "Grams!"

She laughs so hard she almost falls off the barstool.

"What? I like what I like. Maybe you're just being a prude because you don't have anyone special in your life, on the beach or otherwise."

I roll my eyes and grab a rag, wiping down the counter. Not this again. She's been on my case about settling down ever since I moved to Rosewood a few months ago.

After twelve years in the Marines, I was restless and ready for the next chapter of my life. The only problem? I have no idea what that is. I was aimless for a few months until my Grams called me up and said she was finally ready to retire.

She's owned this pub, The Pink Door, for over fifty years. My gramps died nearly a decade ago, but Connie Wolf is nothing if not resilient. She kept up the place until just last month, conveniently right when I was looking for something new. Nothing with Grams is a coincidence, though. I'm sure it was her plan all along to sell me The Pink Door whenever she deemed me worthy of it.

"Give me some time, Grams. It's a small town, you know. Not a whole lot of options."

"Horseshit."

I grin and look over at her, those blue eyes sparkling with mischief. "Getting sassy in your old age?" I tease.

"Old? Good thing I love you, boy, otherwise I'd roll over your toes with my walker. Besides, I'm not wrong. You need someone in your life. All you do is work at the bar and then go upstairs and sleep in your apartment. It's sad."

"Need I remind you that you're the one who sold me the bar and apartment?"

I look at my watch, seeing it's just past three in the afternoon. I suppose that's as good a time as any to have a drink. Especially if Grams wants to talk about my love life. Eyeing the Jack Daniels, I consider pouring myself a shot.

"Don't day drink," Grams scolds. "It's unbecoming." I look at the glass of red wine in her hand and then back at her. "Wine doesn't count."

"Whatever you say, Grams." I shake my head, but I'm smiling the whole time. She's got so much energy and she really does mean well, even when she's giving me shit.

"Come here, Hudson." Her voice is softer now, more serious. I step around the bar and sit on the stool next to her. Grams takes my hand in both of hers, a rare soft smile graces her face. "You know I just don't want you to be all alone when I'm gone."

"You're not going anywhere any time soon," I say, trying to lighten the mood. I don't want to even think about losing Grams.

"I'll try my damndest to live forever, but time makes fools of us all," she says with a wink as she squeezes my hand. "With your parents gone, God rest their souls, and my sweet Steve joining them ten years ago, the pickin's are slim for family around here."

"I have a brother, you know. Slater? You remember him? Seven feet tall, wide as a tank?"

"Of course, you have Slater. But you know he came back from his last tour scarred in more ways than one. He'll need you whenever he decides to come out of hiding and talk to us again. And you'll need someone to support you."

I nod, thinking about my older brother. We both joined the Marines, but I always knew I'd leave after a few years and do something else with my life. Slater, on the other hand, wanted to make it his career. He was a damn good soldier who was in the wrong place at the wrong time. The Humvee he was driving caught a roadside bomb, killing everyone except Slater. He sustained major injuries and was discharged a while ago, though he hasn't returned any of my calls.

I was about ready to fly out to Chicago and tear the city apart looking for him, but then I got a call from his old military buddy, Colton. He and their other friend, Logan, have been checking in on him. The three of them started their own security company, from what I hear. Watchdog Protection. I'd love to visit and tell him how proud I am of the progress he's made, but I think Slater needs to be the one to reach out first. Otherwise, it might be seen as an ambush. Still, I miss him. I wish he'd let me in, or hell, even give me a call.

"We'll cross that bridge when we come to it," I tell Grams.

"Or," she pipes up, the sparkle back in her clear blue eyes. "We can prepare for it now. Make sure you have a good, loyal woman by your side. You say it's a small town, but I don't think you've been looking for your soul mate very hard."

"You got me there," I say sarcastically as I stand up and go back behind the bar. "Besides, I'm still getting used to running things around here. I have a few projects I need to work on to get things up to code." I give her a pointed look, but she just rolls her eyes and waves my concern away.

"Harold doesn't mind. He knows it's all just technicalities. I was running this bar when he was still in diapers. Just because he's the fire chief doesn't mean he knows everything."

"Right, but he might know a thing or two about fire safety." Grams glares at me, but I continue. "Plus, I need to clear out the back room for more storage, research new appliances to update the kitchen, and, no offense, but the decor needs a bit of a facelift."

Grams feigns outrage, but she can't keep it together for long. Her rich laughter fills the bar, making me smile. "Yes, yes, child. I told you it was yours to do with what you please. I know it's a little outdated, but I didn't want to fix anything up only to have you undo it and put something else in place."

I grin and shake my head. The woman drives me crazy sometimes, but at least life is never boring.

"So then you understand how busy I'll be the next few months. It's not a good time to start a relationship. Maybe next year, when things calm down."

"Love doesn't fit into your five-year plan, Hudson. Love comes when it comes, and if you miss it, you might not get a second chance."

"Love? I thought we were just talking about dating." I rub my temples, looking more seriously at the bottle of Jack. It seems Grams isn't going to let this go easily.

"Yes, love. You're not into casual relationships. With you, it's all or nothing. Just like your grandpa."

She's right, of course. I don't know about the all-or-nothing part, but I've never been one for casual relationships, and I don't do one night stands. I never really thought about why, but I suppose what Grams says rings true. I don't want to play games or cycle through women and heartbreaks.

"Even if that's true, it doesn't change the fact that I don't have time." My voice is harsher than I meant it to be. I guess this subject is more sensitive than I thought it was.

Truthfully, it would be amazing to have a partner, someone to share the burden, someone I can support and love. I want the kind of marriage my grandparents had. They were deliriously happy and in love. My deepest fear is that no one will ever measure up. I don't think I could settle for anything less than the all-consuming love I witnessed between Grams and Gramps growing up.

"You'll make time for the right person. I think you'll be amazed at how your priorities change when you've found your soulmate."

"I can't speak to that one way or the other, but I still don't have time to go searching for *the one*. She's not likely to waltz in the door and throw herself at me."

Grams smirks, which is a dangerous thing. "I'll make you a bet."

"Uh-oh."

"Put your money where your mouth is, boy."

"Grams—"

"The next woman to walk through the door and order a shepherd's pie will be your wife."

I laugh, nearly doubling over at her outlandish suggestion. Then I look up and see that she's serious.

"Grams, that's ridiculous. But it's highly specific. The shepherd's pie isn't very popular, and I don't think I've had anyone other than Nathanial Jones order it."

"So, we're on, then?" Before she finishes her sentence, she grabs my wrist, turning toward her so she can check the time. "Come on, boy. Humor me."

"What's the rush? I don't think anyone is going to come in ordering shepherd's pie today. Sorry, Grams."

"Then what's the harm?" Her voice is borderline shrill, but I don't know if it's excitement or nerves. It's hard to tell with Connie Wolf. "Woman. Shepherd's pie. Wife. It's a simple bet."

"What will I get when I win?"

"No need to discuss the stakes. Getting the woman of your dreams is the greatest prize there is."

I sigh and rub a hand down my face. She's not making any sense, but I know I won't get a moment of peace until I give in. "Fine," I breathe out exasperatedly.

"Yes? That's a yes?" She's leaning over the bar, her eyes wide, her smile stretching across her face. If her hips weren't in such bad shape, I have no doubt she'd be bouncing in her seat.

"Yes, but like I said..."

The bell above the door rings, and as if on cue, the most gorgeous woman I've ever seen steps inside. She blinks rapidly, adjusting to the dim lighting here. It's one of the things I want to upgrade.

She has dark, silky brown hair that flows over one shoulder, high cheekbones, a cute little nose, and the lightest green eyes I've ever seen. As she walks toward the bar, I can't help but notice the sway of her wide hips with each step. It takes a considerable amount of effort not to stare at her chest, but Jesus, she's full and curvy everywhere. I want to palm her breasts, squeeze her ass, press her against me, and feel her skin on my skin.

Fuck, what's wrong with me?

Grams smacks my arm, breaking the spell. She gives me a sharp look and tilts her head in the direction of the curvy goddess.

"Hey," I choke out. "Hi. Hello." What is wrong with me? It's like I've never spoken to another living soul.

The woman smiles, her cheeks turning a delicate shade of pink as she tucks some of her glossy hair behind her ear. She's adorable.

"Hey. Hi. Hello," she says softly. I chuckle.

"Welcome to The Pink Door. What can I get for you?" A back rub? A full-body massage? Maybe an orgasm or three? *Get it together!* I scold myself.

"Well I was actually hoping to pick up some shepherd's pie for—"

My good mood vanishes in an instant. "Shepherd's pie?" I cut her off, then glare at Grams, who is looking at me with wide, disapproving eyes. "I should have been expecting you."

"Oh, that's okay," the beautiful but scheming woman says, confusion coloring her words. She's a good actress, I'll give her that much. "Um, so am I able to get the pie then? It's for—"

"I know what it's for." I'm practically growling, but I can't seem to help it. My grams set me up, and this gorgeous angel is in on it. I'm trying not to be upset with her. I know how persuasive my grandma can be.

"I... I-I'm sorry," the woman says, taking a few steps back. "I'm not sure what you're talking about." Her green eyes shine with hurt, which does something funny to my chest. It feels like it's caving in. But what did she expect? That I'd fall for the most obvious set-up in the world?

"That's a lie," I mutter.

"Hudson Wolf! You apologize right now!" Grams says, smacking my arm again.

"It's okay," the woman says, taking another step back. "It's probably best that I go."

"Good idea," I grunt, though the words taste bitter in my mouth. Is it so wrong to want this woman to want me for me and not because my grandma sold her on some happily ever after with her perfect grandson?

"Hudson!" Grams barks out at me.

"I'm going, I'm going." The woman spins on her heel, stumbling over a loose board. I rush out from behind the bar to help her. I may be frustrated, but I'm not cruel. I'm not going to let her get hurt because of my grandma's schemes.

She rights herself before I reach her, looking at me over her shoulder. Her captivating eyes latch onto mine for half a second, and I feel like an asshole. She looks genuinely alarmed and confused.

Before I get a chance to say anything, the brown-haired angel is gone, leaving the door swinging behind her.

"I can't believe you!" Grams shouts from her seat at the bar.

"Me? I can't believe *you*! You didn't think I'd actually fall for that, right?"

"I thought you weren't a rude little shit, and I had no idea you'd kick the poor girl out." I roll my eyes, though I do feel a little bad about how I reacted. "Especially since she has no clue what's going on."

"What?" Now it's my turn to spin on my heel and gape and Grams. "What do you mean she had no idea? That wasn't actually fate intervening. This has your fingerprints all over it."

"Maybe so, but Sydney didn't have anything to do with it. I may have talked to her grandmother last week. It's possible the two of us thought Sydney would be perfect for you."

"So, let me get this straight," I sigh, scrubbing my hands down my face. "Both of you plotted to get us together, without telling either of us, and this is the plan you came up with?" Grams nods. At least she has the decency to look a little sheepish. "And I just yelled at the most beautiful woman I've ever met?"

"And called her a liar. And kicked her out," Grams adds, unhelpfully.

I scowl at her, but then realize what an ass I've been. That's not like me at all. I'm generally easy-going, but I just showed this Sydney woman the worst side of me.

"What are you waiting for, boy?"

"What do you mean?" I look up at Grams, who has a knowing smile firmly in place.

"Go get your girl, you fool!"

"Shit," I groan, running out the door. At the very least, I need to apologize. And maybe steal a kiss. And take her on a date. And wake up with her every morning. "Shit," I mutter again, not sure what to make of these feelings. All I know is that I messed up and I need to make it better.

Chapter Two

Sydney

What the flipping heck is happening?

"Wait! Miss! Come back!"

I look over my shoulder to see the man from the bar chasing me. I snort out a laugh at the thought of Mr. Tall, Dark, and Handsome chasing after me for a different reason. I hardly got a look at him before he got upset and called me a liar. Still, it was enough time to notice the way his muscles filled out his tight white t-shirt. With dark hair, a sharp jaw, and eyes as blue as a clear day in Rosewood, there's no denying the man is gorgeous.

And crazy. And rude. And chasing me down after kicking me out of his bar.

"Sydney! Wait!"

How does he know my name? And why won't he go away? I left, just like he wanted.

My cute ballerina flats slide a bit on the concrete as I pick up speed, but I manage to keep from toppling over. It's been ages since I've run. The last time was probably in high school when they made us do the mile run as a fitness test. I almost puked before I even finished.

"No, thank you," I huff out. Dang, it's hard talking while running. I push through though, needing this man to stop. If I keep this up much longer, I'm going to collapse into a sweaty mess.

"I just want to apologize." Of course, his voice is like honey over gravel. It's somehow smooth and rich, with a gritty undertone.

Still, he was a jerk, and I have no idea why! My grandma asked me to pick up a shepherd's pie from The Pink Door. It was a little odd since I don't think I've seen her eat red meat in years, but she wants what she wants, and I want to get it for her.

The man's footsteps are closer now, and I can hear each inhale and exhale. Why does that make me break out into goosebumps? Why is my stomach all tied up? My heart thumps unevenly against my ribcage and my chest grows tight.

Oh, Lordy, am I about to have a panic attack?

"I don't like being yelled at the first time I walk inside a restaurant," I shout at the man quickly gaining on me. I tend to ramble when I'm rattled, and that whole experience was upsetting, to say the least. "Maybe the third or fourth time," I continue for literally no reason except that I can't stop. "But first impressions matter, you know? Is this how you treat all of your customers? How are you still open?"

Shut up, shut up, shut up!

Anxiety grips me in its clutches, squeezing the air from my lungs until I'm dizzy. For some reason, my messed-up brain translates this panicky, suffocating feeling into blurting out whatever is on my mind. I feel the words bubbling up inside of me, and I try to swallow them down.

The tall, broad, jerky hunk is hot on my heels. He laughs, and I'm pretty sure it's at my expense. My face burns with embarrassment. How did a simple errand turn into this crazy mess?

Up ahead, I see the sign for The Grind Cafe. *Hallelujah.* I can slip inside, run to the bathroom, and lock the door behind me. Maybe there's a window I can crawl out of.

The door to the cafe swings open, and I narrowly avoid Dr. Martin as he steps outside.

"Sydney!" he exclaims.

"Sorry!" I murmur, dashing farther inside.

Dr. Martin looks at me, then looks at the gorgeous, rude bartender with narrowed eyes. The man puts his hands out in front of him in a sign of surrender. I turn my back on him and head down the hall, toward the restroom.

"Holy moly," I whisper as I grip the sides of the sink to hold myself up.

Taking a few calming breaths, I close my eyes and try to center myself. When I open them again, I stare into the mirror, taking in my flushed cheeks, wide eyes, and trembling lips. I always get the shakes when I'm worked up like this. I don't even know what happened or why that man was so upset and then so adamant about apologizing. It doesn't make sense.

After splashing some cold water on my face, I feel a little more like myself. I could go for a drink right about now, and not an alcoholic one. Definitely not one from The Pink Door. Tea is more my jam.

I step up to the counter and order my drink then wait off to the side with the other customers. I focus on taking deep, even breaths. I've lived with anxiety for most of my life. Ever since a house fire claimed both of my parents when I was four. I was trapped in my room until a firefighter broke in and saved me.

Sometimes, I can still feel the heat on my skin, the kind of heat that burns instantly and then makes you numb. Rubbing the jagged scar on my forehead, I close my eyes and work through a breathing exercise my grandma taught me. I used to wake up screaming and thrashing, trying to fight my way out of my room. My grandma stayed by my side and rocked me back to sleep each time.

It's been years since I've had a nightmare like that, but the suffocating feeling never left me. It gets worse when I'm in crowds or when I open my mouth and blurt out something stupid.

"Sydney!"

I turn toward the friendly, familiar voice. "Hey, Evan!"

One of my best friends, Evangeline, aka Evan, makes her way over to me and wraps me up in a hug. "I love bumping into you around town again," she says with a smile.

"I know! I missed you so much when I was away at college."

"Agreed."

The barista calls out my drink, and I grab it, thanking her.

"Uh-oh," Evan says. "Is that chamomile tea? What's wrong?"

I sigh and let her lead me to a nearby table. Evan and I grew up together here in Rosewood, Colorado, along with our other bestie, Rowan. If anyone knows what chamomile tea means, it'd be Evan.

"Spill!" Evan says as soon as we sit down.

"I'm fine, really," I insist, stirring some honey into my tea.

"Uh, no you're not. You just poured a cup of honey in there. This is definitely not nothing."

I narrow my eyes at her, but she just smiles, knowing she's won.

"I had a... weird encounter at The Pink Door," I start, staring down into my tea.

"Oh yeah? Hudson just bought the place from his grandma."

"Hudson. So that's the jerk's name," I mutter, gripping my cup harder than necessary.

"Jerk? Hudson? He's usually pretty chill, always has a smile for everyone."

"Not the man I met."

"Tall? Wide shoulders? Scruffy black hair and blue eyes?"

"Yup, that's the one."

"What happened?"

I take a long sip of my drink, letting the hot liquid warm me up and soothe my nerves. "Well, my grandma wanted a shepherd's pie from The Pink Door. She was very adamant that they have the best shepherd's pie. I walked into the bar, and at first, Hudson seemed nice. Flustered maybe, but nice." I remember his stuttered-out greeting, which I thought was adorable. Until he opened his mouth again. "Anyway, I asked for the shepherd's pie, and it was like a flip switched. He called me a liar and basically kicked me out."

"What? What the hell?"

"And *then*, he chased me down the sidewalk! At first, I thought it was to make sure I stayed far away, but then he yelled something about an apology. It was all too much, you know? I don't know what I did, but I couldn't handle another encounter with him. That's when I ran in here and nearly plowed into Dr. Martin."

Evan tilts her head to the side, a sympathetic look on her face. I used to think she was pitying me because of my sometimes crippling anxiety, but now I know she's just concerned. It's my pesky anxiety that tried convincing me Evan and Rowan didn't really like me and only hung out with me because they felt bad for the socially awkward nerd in school. Nothing could be further from the truth, but it took a while to trust them and their friendship.

"Maybe he was just having a bad day?" Evan muses. I shrug, busying myself with drinking my tea. "Or... you know, this whole thing reeks of two meddling old ladies."

"What do you mean?"

"Well, you know how your grandma is," she says with a grin.

"Yes, she's gotten quite feisty these days," I agree, rolling my eyes playfully. Darla Reese is a character, that's for sure. As soon as she found her first gray hair, she decided to dye it all pink. And then lavender. And then fire engine red. Her current color is teal, which she's had for a while now. Her personality is as bright and bold as her hair.

"Well, she might have met her match in Hudson's grandma, Connie Wolf."

"Connie Wolf..." I remember her from before I left for college. She was sweet, a little nosey, but overall a genuinely nice person. Everyone here in Rosewood is. Well, except Hudson, apparently.

"Yeah. She's been teaming up with your grandma lately and getting into all sorts of trouble," Evan informs me. She was the only one out of our friend group who stayed behind in Rosewood. Both Rowan and I went off to college, though we're all back in the same town now.

"Okay, so what does that have to do anything?"

"I'm just saying, your grandma sending you to Hudson's bar, Hudson flipping out... I don't know. Something is off. Like I said, that doesn't sound like the Hudson I know. He hasn't been in town long, but he seems like a decent, cheery guy."

"So it's just me then. Good to know."

Evan reaches across the table and covers my hand with hers. "Is that what you really think, or is that the anxiety talking?"

I frown at her, not liking how well she can read me. Evan just smiles sweetly, reassuringly, before giving my hand one last squeeze.

"Anyway, tell me about you. How's your man doing?"

Evan's whole face brightens, her smile turning absolutely radiant. She recently found her happily ever after with the guy she's been crushing on for years. I'm so happy for her, and for Rowan, too. Rowan has had a rough couple of months raising her daughter on her own, but Reed came back into their lives and now my besties have loving partners.

I listen to Evan tell me about how happy she is and her new thriving business, The Garden Goddess. I'm overjoyed for my friends. They are the best, most loyal people I know, but I'd be lying if I said jealousy didn't creep in every once in a while. Like now. Evan is positively beaming as she gestures with her hands. I keep my smile firmly in place, but I can't help the twinge of envy deep in my chest.

I don't know if I'll ever find someone to love me as much as Rowan and Evan's men love them. For starters, I'm a big girl. My friends are both curvy as well, but they've always seemed elegant and confident. Me, on the other hand... not so much. My body image was at an all-time low in high school, but Rowan and Evan taught me to make peace with my curves. I still struggle to accept myself as beautiful no matter what size, though. It's hard not to.

And then there's the fact that I can hardly hold a conversation with a man. Even Ted, the checkout guy at Rosewood Market, makes me nervous. He's fifty-five and happily married with three kids. Yet, I can hardly look him in the eye. How will I ever talk to someone long enough for them to fall in love with me if I can't even do that much?

Plus, my scar bothers me so much I tend to keep my head down, letting my long hair cover up as much of the marred flash as possible. Suffice it to say, I'm not very approachable, and even if someone did approach me, I'm sure I'd scare them off.

Evangeline checks her watch and then hops up, telling me she has to get back to work. We make plans to meet up with Rowan later in the week, and then she leaves me alone with my thoughts.

As much as I don't want to admit it, my mind keeps wandering back to Hudson Wolf. Dang, the man is fine. The kind of striking, rugged beauty I've only seen on the big screen. But Hudson is real flesh and blood. And he also doesn't like me.

I sigh and shake my head, dispelling my thoughts. I finish up my tea and head home, hoping to put this day behind me.

Chapter Three

Hudson

My eyes fly open and my heart thunders in my chest. *What the hell woke me up?*

Then I hear it again. Someone is trying to break down my door from the sounds of it. I leap out of bed, groaning when I see what time it is. Six-fucking-forty on a Saturday morning. Throwing on a pair of old jeans and a t-shirt, I run to the door before it splinters apart.

When I open it, I'm greeted by Grams. She's scowling at me. Not a great way to start the weekend.

"Did you hurt yourself trying to break in?" I grumble as I let her inside.

"No, dear. My walker makes for a good battering ram."

Despite my annoyance, I crack a smile at her. I really do love the woman, even when she's driving me up a fucking wall.

"What are you doing here, Grams? Everything okay?"

"I'm not the one you should be worried about," she snips out once she's comfortable on the couch.

I rub the sleep out of my eyes and take a deep breath. "I'm not awake enough to play these games. Who should I be worried about?"

"Your future wife!" she says in a huff.

"We went over this yesterday," I groan while getting out the coffee grounds and filling up the pot. I'm going to need caffeine for this conversation. "I tried apologizing but she ran into The Grind, and I was cut off by Dr. Martin."

"And that's it? You're not going to try to win her over? Where is your spirit, boy? Your sense of adventure?"

I'm glad my back is facing Grams, otherwise, she might see the regret on my face. Truthfully, I had a terrible night's sleep thanks to a guilty conscience. When I wasn't berating myself for being an ass, I was picturing Sydney's green eyes, pouty lips, and thick, curvaceous body.

"How do you suppose I'll win her over? If I was interested in that," I mumble. Peering over my shoulder, I see Grams's eyes go wide, and then a dangerous smile spreads across her face. *This can't be good.*

"For starters, you could actually apologize."

I turn around and lean against the counter while the coffee brews. "I tried that yesterday. She wasn't very receptive."

"Well, can you blame the poor girl? She had a six-and-a-half-foot stranger chasing her down the street, for goodness sake!"

"Grams! You're the one who told me to go after her!"

"I guess I assumed you'd have a bit more charm."

"What's that supposed to mean? And how do you know I wasn't charming yesterday?"

"I got a call from Darla last night," she says casually while looking over her freshly painted fingernails.

"Darla Reese? Sydney's grandma and the other half of your matchmaking catastrophe?"

"Oh, hush. It's not a catastrophe. Not yet. It all depends on you."

"No pressure," I grumble, pouring two cups of coffee.

"Yes, pressure!" Grams says exasperatedly. "Darla said Sydney wasn't herself all evening. Something about having a bad day with anxiety. It doesn't take a genius to figure out what might have caused that."

"Anxiety?" My chest grows tight, and my stomach ties itself in knots. I knew I was rude, but I tried making it up to her. Then again, Grams is right. Having a stranger chase you down after they kicked you out isn't exactly the best way to get the point across.

Grams must see the guilt written all over my face. Her gaze softens, and she sets her mug down on the side table, covering my hand with hers. "It's not my place to say, but—"

I cut her off with a chuckle. "Not your place to say? Why, Grams, I don't think I've ever heard those words come out of your mouth."

She smirks at me and rolls her eyes. "Well, this is different. Sydney is special."

I nod my head and take another sip of coffee. She's right, of course. That's the thing about my grams. She's feisty, gossipy, and unconventional, but she tends to be right about most things. She knows it, too.

"I agree. But what can I do about it now? I already yelled at her, kicked her out, and nearly gave her a panic attack. I don't know how to fix that."

"But you want to?"

"Yeah, of course. I don't like the way things ended between us."

"And…?" Grams tilts her head forward, both eyebrows raised as she stares at me expectantly.

"And…" I sigh and scrub a hand down my face. "And she's the most beautiful woman I've ever met, and I'd regret not having a second chance with her."

"I know." Grams looks very pleased with herself at my admission.

Leaning back in my chair, I finish off my coffee, feeling a little more like myself. "So, what do you suggest?"

"I'm so glad you asked!" She claps her hands and wiggles around in her seat. *Lord, send me strength for whatever she has cooked up.*

"Now, Grams, don't go overboard here. I get the feeling that Sydney would be embarrassed by grand gestures, especially if they make a public scene."

"You're good for her already! Just a sec, I have to tell Darla what you just said." Grams pulls out her phone and starts texting her best friend. I have to grin at her. I got her an iPhone for Christmas last year, and she loves it. Knows more about it than I do. "Okay, she's been updated. Now. Darla told me something interesting last night. She said Sydney likes to go to the Rosewood Market on Saturday mornings. She gets there early and then treats herself to coffee and a pastry after.

Wouldn't it be wonderful if you bumped into her at the market and took her out for coffee?"

"That sounds an awful lot like stalking," I muse. The absolute, batshit crazy thing is, I'm not against it. The more I think about the confusion and hurt in Sydney's bottomless green eyes, the harder it is to breathe. She was scared of me, or at the very least, wary. I don't like that one bit. If I have to stalk her a bit to prove to her I'm a good man, then so be it. Only me, though. If anyone else stalked my woman, I'd knock them the fuck out.

Oh no.

My woman? When did that happen?

Grams smiles at me like she knows exactly what I'm thinking. "Something tells me you don't mind. Now, chop-chop! Sydney will be at Rosewood Market by seven-thirty!"

I check the time and jump out of my chair before helping Grams off the couch and escorting her out. It's just past seven, and I still need to shower and make myself presentable. Sydney said first impressions are important. I hope second impressions can make up for horrible first ones.

Thirty minutes later, I'm walking into Rosewood Market, wiping my sweaty palms on my jeans. I've never been this nervous around a woman, or at all, for that matter. Twelve years in the Marines has made me immune to the curveballs life throws my way. Until Sydney.

Now, all I can think about is how badly I screwed up. I'll need to be gentle with her and choose my words wisely. I'll show Sydney I'm not really a jerk, just a dumbass.

Grabbing a basket from up front, I stroll down the first aisle I see, trying to be as casual as possible. What was I thinking, letting Grams talk me into this? I don't even need anything from the store, but I should probably put some things in my basket otherwise I'll look suspicious.

I wander up one aisle and down the next, picking up some applesauce and popcorn along the way. Turning the corner, I stop dead in my tracks when I see the angel with brown hair. Her back is facing me, and she's up on her tiptoes trying to grab a jar of salsa.

Rushing over to her, I reach above Sydney's head and snag the salsa before backing off and handing it to her.

"Oh, thank..." Sydney trails off once her eyes meet mine.

I can't breathe for a second with all of her attention focused on me. How is she more beautiful than I remember? Believe me, I pictured her all night last night, but the fantasy isn't even close to the real thing.

She has her hair in a braid today, which lays over one shoulder, making her look so damn sweet. Her porcelain cheeks turn pink, and she licks her bottom lip, though I don't think she's even aware of it.

"You."

I'm not sure if she's finishing her thanks or if she's accusing me of being myself. Probably the latter.

"You," I echo back, smiling at her. I hope to disarm the curvy little goddess.

Sydney dips her head down, readjusting the items in her basket and placing the salsa inside. I notice her hand shake slightly, and I want to kick myself.

"Can we start over?" I ask softly. Sydney slowly lifts her gaze to meet mine, the most adorably puzzled look on her face. When she nods, I stick out my hand for her to shake. She stares at it for a second, and then tentatively places her delicate hand in my rough one. "Hey. Hi. Hello."

Sydney graces me with the most precious smile, her green eyes sparkling as she remembers my stuttered-out greeting from yesterday. Yes, that's where I want to pick up. That moment she whispered the words back to me and blushed so sweetly. The moment before I fucked it up and accused her of lying.

"Hey. Hi. Hello," she murmurs, just like yesterday.

"I'm Hudson Wolf, and I think we got started off on the wrong foot. You said first impressions matter, but what about second impressions?"

I'm still holding her hand, and she makes no move to pull away. Jesus, her warmth, her smooth skin, and the fact that she's so much smaller than me make me want to scoop her up and take her home with me.

Sydney is shorter than I remember. Then again, I didn't get this close to her yesterday. She has to be five three or four, almost a foot shorter than I am. But her curves... there's nothing tiny about her hips, ass, or chest, and I fucking love it. I didn't know I had a type, but I've never met Sydney. She's my type.

"Second impressions are a lot like first impressions," she finally whispers. Her voice is so soft, I have to lean in to hear her. Do I really make her that nervous? I'll have to be careful with my Sydney if I want to bring her out of her shell. "Everybody gets one."

I grin at her, thrilled when she grins back. "I like that policy. I'd like to officially make a second impression, if that's alright with you."

Sydney nods and my heart nearly beats out of my chest. *Don't fuck it up*, the voice in the back of my head reminds me.

"So far, this one is much better." She nibbles on her bottom lip, driving me insane with the need to do the same. I want to pull that juicy lip through my teeth and then claim her mouth as my own, kissing her until she melts into me and feels how perfect we are together.

I clear my throat and try to control my lust. Easier said than done. "Good."

Sydney looks down at our entwined hands. Somehow, we went from shaking hands to holding hands, her fingers interlaced with mine. I give her a squeeze and she pulls her hand back, much to my disappointment. My skin still tingles from her touch. I'm already addicted.

"So, um..." She looks down and then to the side. Anywhere but at me. It's clear that she's uncomfortable, but I don't think it's with me, necessarily. More the situation.

"You come here often?" I ask, hoping to lighten the mood.

My breath catches in my throat when she rewards me with another smile at my cheesy pickup line. "Well, considering it's one of two places to buy groceries in Rosewood, yeah, I'm here often."

We fall into a light conversation as I follow her around like a puppy dog. Sydney grabs a few things, seemingly more comfortable with something to do while she talks to me. I don't mind. One day soon, I hope she won't be so anxious around me.

"Is that all you're getting?" she asks, staring at my basket with two measly items.

"Yeah, I don't need much," I say with a wink. Sydney blushes and darts her eyes away. God, she's adorable.

"But... why did you hang out with me the entire time if you didn't need anything else?" The genuine confusion kills me. Does she really not know how enchanting she is?

"I did need something else. More time with you." I give her another wink, and this time, my girl rolls her eyes. I love seeing a bit more of her personality shine through.

"That's almost as bad as the 'you come here often' line. You need new material, mister."

I chuckle and guide her to one of two registers, my hand lightly grazing her lower back. Sydney shivers but doesn't move away from me. I know I have to take it slow, but dammit, all I want to do is pull her against me and taste her sweetness on my tongue.

"I guess I'm out of practice. It got a smile out of you though, so I'll consider it a win."

Sydney doesn't say anything, and I don't expect her to. I know today was a lot for her. We step up in line, and I panic about my time being up. I need to ask her out to coffee, but I'm not sure how. It's been over a decade since I've asked someone out.

The cashier starts to ring up Sydney's groceries and I look around the store, trying to think of some way to draw her back into conversation. Spotting a newly renovated part of the store, I comment on the bright green shelves and orange tiles.

"Reminds me of a carrot," I blurt out awkwardly. Ted, the cashier, raises his eyebrows at my words. Sydney looks up at me, her brows furrowed. "The new health section," I clarify, tipping my head in that direction.

"Oh yeah," Sydney giggles a bit. It's the lightest, purest sound I've ever heard. "It kind of does."

Relieved that my odd topic of conversation seemed to work, I gain a bit more confidence. "I bet they spent a pretty penny hiring an interior designer. Not that it did any good. I mean, look at that mess! I know next to nothing about all that stuff, but even I can see the green and orange clash."

I chuckle and look down at Sydney, who is digging around in her purse to pay for her groceries. Her shoulders are slumped and she refuses to look at me. Fuck, what did I say?

"I can get your groceries," I offer, hoping to make it up to her.

Sydney shakes her head no, still not meeting my eyes. She quickly swipes her card and gathers up her bags, rushing out the door. I set my basket down and start to chase her again, but Ted stops me.

"Whoa there, Hudson."

"I'll put my groceries back in a second, I just need to get to Sydney," I insist. "She was upset with me, right?" I honestly don't know where it all went wrong.

"Let me give you a hint," Ted says, crossing his arms over his chest. "Sydney recently moved back to town after getting her degree. In interior design."

"Fuck," I growl, wiping a hand down my face. What is wrong with me? I should have asked her more about herself and what brought her back to Rosewood. Actually, I should have shut my mouth and not tried to be clever. That doesn't seem to work on Sydney. Then another thought occurs. "Wait, she didn't design the new health section, did she?"

"No, thankfully you didn't mess up that much."

A humorless laugh leaves my mouth. "Damn. I can't seem to get anything right when it comes to that woman."

I rub my chest with the heel of my hand, right over my heart. It's beating rapidly, a tightness expanding throughout my body with each erratic thump-thump-thump.

"Be patient. She's always been..." Ted hesitates, and I narrow my eyes at him. If he says one disparaging word about Sydney, I might have to punch him in the face. I don't care if he's in his mid-fifties. "Shy," he finishes, with a soft look in his eyes. It's clear the man is just watching out for Sydney.

"That's what I hear. I managed to screw up twice with her, and I'm not so sure she'll give me another chance."

"Flirting about the color of the walls isn't a great start," he says with a smirk. "I've been out of the game for decades, and even I know that."

"Yeah, yeah," I grumble.

"So, do you want your applesauce and popcorn?"

I consider putting them back, but that would take too much time. I need to figure out another way to talk to Sydney. Pulling out my wallet, I hand Ted a twenty and tell him to keep the change.

Sydney said everyone gets one second impression. I hope she feels the same way about third impressions.

Chapter Four

Sydney

A heavy sigh leaves my lips as I finish up yet another job application. I've been at it for three hours and I can feel the life source draining out of me. There are only so many ways you can dress up "I'm a recent college grad with years of training but no actual experience" without lying. I think I've found every one of them.

"Why the frown?" my grandma asks as she enters the dining room.

Her teal hair is teased up into a modern-ish beehive and she has on her white horned-rimmed glasses with red jewels on the corners. Her clothes clash and her socks don't match. She's absolutely beautiful. I hope I'm half as lively as my grandma when I'm her age. Heck, I could use some of that liveliness now.

"More applications," I whine overdramatically before resting my forehead on the table. "They want people who are young enough to understand branding and have fresh ideas, yet also someone who has fifteen years of experience."

My grandma takes a seat next to me and pats me on the head. "Have you considered not working for someone else?"

"What?" I lift my head up and raise an eyebrow at her.

"You know, like start your own interior design business. I saw you discussing paint colors with the neighbors last weekend when they were redoing their guest room. I know you've been over there several times this week to offer more advice. And just yesterday, you were giving Mrs. Carmella advice on the best tile for her basement. This stuff is in your blood, babycakes," she says, tucking a strand of hair behind my ear.

"But..." I honestly never thought that was a possibility, at least not at this stage in my life. It would be kind of amazing to set my own schedule and only choose projects I'm passionate about.

But of course, I can't do that. I'm twenty-one and I don't have any money for start-up costs. While I value my education, I've never done a paid gig, so how could I possibly expect anyone to hire me with my severely lacking portfolio?

"Are you thinking of all the reasons it won't work out?" My grandma is a little too perceptive for my liking.

"No," I say in the least convincing voice ever. She gives me *the look*, the one that says she knows you're full of BS. "Fine. Maybe a little. But they are valid reasons. I need experience, for one thing. And money."

"What if you had those things? Would you consider working for yourself?"

"No." My response is immediate, and I say it so forcefully I think I shocked myself as much as my grandma. "I didn't realize I was so against it until right now. I just... I think I need to go be around other designers for a while. Blend in and observe with an entry-level job. And I guess we'll see where things go from there."

My grandmother nods her head, considering my words. Then, she cups my hand in both of hers and takes a deep breath.

"My sweet granddaughter," she says softly. "You are stronger than you know. I've watched you quite literally rise from the ashes and take life head-on. Yes, you've had setbacks, and yes, anxiety is ever-present. But those things don't get to define you. That's the beauty of life. You get to choose how to live it."

I sniffle and wipe away a rogue tear. "Thank you," I whisper. "But that still doesn't change the part where I'm young and inexperienced."

She tilts her head to the side and studies me for a moment. My grandmother often surprises people with how perceptive she is. She's not just bright hair and eclectic clothing. She's intuitive and sharp as a tack.

"Just promise me this, Sydney. Promise you'll choose your future based on your hopes, not your fears."

My grandma gives my hand one last squeeze, then stands and kisses the top of my head before stepping out of the room. Her words sink deeper and deeper, taking root in my soul. What do I hope for? What do I fear?

That second question is easy to answer. I fear the unknown. Small spaces. Big crowds. Loud noises. Being the center of attention. Is that the real reason starting my own business sounds so terrifying?

My phone rings, startling me out of my downward spiral. I look down and see Rowan's name flash across the screen. Smiling, I pick it up.

"Hey! What's up?"

"Sydney! What are you doing tonight?"

"Probably whatever you're going to ask me to do," I say with a laugh. "Do you need me to babysit Harper?"

"No, Reed is on daddy duty tonight. I was hoping for a girl's night? We could go to The Pink Door and grab some drinks?"

"What? No!"

"Uh... no to the girl's night?"

"No, I mean yes. No. Ugh!" I pinch the bridge of my nose and try taking a controlled breath.

"Everything okay, Syd?"

"Yes. No."

Rowan laughs. "Okay then, thanks for clearing that up."

"Sorry, I'm a little scatter-brained right now. Girl's night would be amazing. Just not at The Pink Door."

"Oh-kaaayyy... that sounds like a story I need to hear."

"I'll tell you while we're stuffing our faces at Little Star Pizza. Say six o'clock?"

"You little tease!" she jokes. "Six it is. I'm glad you're back in town, Syd."

"Me too. Give Harper a kiss from me!"

We say our goodbyes, and I stare at the clock. I suppose I could do a few more applications before getting ready to see the girls.

***

"Oh my gosh! You guys look so happy together!" I swoon over the photos Rowan is showing us of her man, Reed, and their precious seven-month-old, Harper.

The adorable little girl was a total surprise to her mom and dad, and while it took a while for Reed and Rowan to work things out, they are now more in love than ever. It's sweet. And it only makes me a *little* jealous.

"I'm just glad I got my hair and makeup to look right. Having a kid is not for the faint of heart," Rowan jokes.

"Things are better with Reed around though, right?" Evan asks.

"Yeah," Rowan sighs, a dreamy smile tugging at her lips. "But enough about me. Let's talk about why you don't want to go to The Pink Door."

I quickly shove a piece of pizza into my mouth to avoid her question.

"Are you talking about Hudson?" Evan exclaims. "Did something else happen?"

"Something *else*? I didn't even know there was some*thing* to begin with! Tell me everything right now, Sydney."

"Your mom voice doesn't work on me," I retort, sticking my tongue out at her. She grabs my pizza slice, holding it hostage. "Fiiinnneeee," I sigh. "But first, pizza."

"Always," Evan agrees.

After demolishing the last piece, I get Rowan caught up on my first encounter with Hudson.

"Okay, so then what happened? Did you see him again?" Rowan asks.

"Was he mean to you? I'll give him a piece of my mind, you just give me the word," Evan says.

"Thanks, but I'll be fine. We bumped into each other at the grocery store. He was... nice, at first. I mean, he startled me, but he was just grabbing the salsa since I couldn't reach the top shelf."

"Aw," Evan coos. Rowan gives her a sharp look.

"Not so fast. I have a feeling there's more."

I nod my head and tell them about the incident from yesterday. I was startled at first to look up into those clear blue eyes. There wasn't any frustration or tension like the day in his bar. No, the Hudson I saw at the market was almost... sweet.

The way he asked if we could start over, and how he recited his opening line from our first encounter. *Hey. Hi. Hello.* I pause in the middle of my story, picturing his lips curling into a soft smile when he shook my hand.

The heat from his touch shot down my spine and made my skin erupt in goosebumps. The entire time he was following me around, I was keenly aware of him. Every time our fingers brushed or he guided me down the aisle with his hand on my lower back, I shivered and had to squeeze my thighs together.

"Okay, lady, what aren't you telling us?" Rowan accuses. "You're blushing and have a glazed-over look in your eye. He must not be so bad if you like him this much."

"I do not like him," I correct her. "Besides, I'm not done yet. Things seemed to be going pretty good, but then when we were waiting in line, he mentioned that the new health section in the Rosewood Market looks like a carrot with the orange tiles and green shelves."

"It totally does," Evan agrees.

"Yeah, that checks out," Rowan says with a nod.

"Right, but that wasn't the problem. Hudson went on to basically say that interior designers are overrated and overpaid."

"What?!" both girls exclaim.

"Yeah." I nod my head and slurp down the rest of my Sprite. "Anyway, I paid for my food and got out of there. I think I heard him calling my name, but I couldn't stand looking at him knowing he thinks my career is a joke."

My friends share a look, and then they each grab one of my hands. "We love you, Sydney," Evan says. "Your career isn't a joke. You've helped me a lot with rearranging stuff at The Garden Goddess to accommodate a better flow of foot traffic. I never would have thought of that."

"Yeah, and remember when I was having trouble with the lighting in my photography studio? You were right there giving me suggestions and you didn't give up until we figured out the solution," Rowan adds.

"Thanks, guys," I say, meaning it with my whole heart. These two may be a few years older than me, but we've always been close. It's times like these, I remember why. "It's dumb. Why should I care what he thinks about me, right?"

"Right," Rowan agrees, nodding her head.

"Yeah," Evan says, though she gives me a look that tells me she doesn't believe me.

"Anyway, that's why I will be avoiding The Pink Door from now on. I lift my mostly empty cup and make a toast. "No more Hudson Wolf, and no more drama."

We clink our plastic cups together, and the girls laugh. I smile with them, but I can't deny the tiny pinprick of pain in my chest at the thought of not seeing Hudson again. What is wrong with me?

Chapter Five

Hudson

"Sydney..." I gasp out her name as I startle awake from another filthy dream about my curvy goddess. "Fuck," I groan, my hand immediately rubbing against the painfully hard bulge in my boxers. I swear I could smell her this time as we moved and came together in a sweaty, trembling mess.

Lying in bed with visions of Sydney's dark hair fanned out across my pillow while I pound into that tight little pussy doesn't exactly help the growing problem in my shorts. I look over at the clock, seeing it's just after seven in the morning. It's as good a time as any to start the day.

Grabbing a towel, I head to the bathroom and strip down before stepping under the hot stream of water. I groan as the droplets slide down my heated, sensitive skin, wishing they were Sydney's fingers. I just know her touch would be gentle yet erotic.

Jesus, I want this woman in an all-consuming, soul-shattering kind of way. Her body, mind, and heart are mine. As soon as I figure out how to get my foot out of my mouth, that is.

Knowing I won't get anything done today with my angry dick in its current position, I give in to the temptation to stroke myself to images of my woman.

I picture licking her nipples into tight, pebbled peaks and dipping my fingers into her dripping wet pussy. I work her up real good and then plunge inside of her, making her take my thick dick in one long stroke.

I grunt, imaging my fingers digging into the soft, creamy skin of Sydney's round hips as I pound away at her, harder, faster, deeper. Squeezing my eyes shut, I picture flipping her onto her stomach and sliding into her from behind.

I reach out and wrap her glossy brown hair around my fist and slam into her again and again. My cock twitches as I pump my hand up and down the now fully hard shaft.

I smack that ass and watch it jiggle for me, her juicy curves making me spurt more precum as I get lost in the fantasy. Faster, faster I stroke myself, nearing my end, but not quite able to reach it. Tightening my grip on Sydney's hair, I tug her head to the side so I can kiss her. I'm met with bright green eyes, burning with just as much desperate passion as I'm feeling. I thrust my hips into my hand and brace my other hand on the shower wall in front of me, grunting with each stroke.

I watch Sydney's pink lips part as she screams out her orgasm. Imagining her chanting my name at the peak of her climax pushes me over the edge.

"*Fucking hell*, Sydney," I roar as my cum shoots out of me in forceful waves and swirls down the drain.

My shoulders slump and I heave out a breath, still shaking from my orgasm. Goddamn. I've never come so hard, and that was only a fantasy. I don't know if I'll survive having the real thing, but there's nothing I won't do to find out. To have her skin sliding against mine, her delicate scent wrapped around me, mixed with our sweat and lovemaking...

I shake my head, clearing those thoughts. I don't have time to jerk off again, and that's exactly where this is heading if I keep it up.

An hour later, I'm at the bar, putting away the new supply order that was dropped off this morning. My mind hasn't strayed from Sydney for a single moment. I've been fumbling around all morning, bumping into things and dropping glasses. This woman has crawled inside my chest, taken hold of my heart, and planted herself deep in my soul. I know I won't be satisfied until I have her as my own.

"Where are we with Operation Wifing Sydney?"

Grams's voice breaks into my reverie. Damn, I think she might want me to be with Sydney almost as much as I do.

"Wifing Sydney, huh? Is that the best you could come up with?"

"I thought I'd make it straight to the point. You seem to have a hard time getting the message across."

"Gee, thanks," I mutter, though I still grin. She's ridiculous, and I love her for it.

"Tell me about the market. Did you get a coffee date? Did she go to your place? Oh, Hudson, am I going to be a great grandmother soon?"

"Jesus, Grams," I chuckle. "No, I didn't sleep with Sydney on the first date."

"But there was a date?" she asks excitedly.

I sigh and shake my head no. "Not exactly." Grams deflates and then scowls at me. "It started out well..." I trail off, remembering Sydney's hesitancy to talk to me at first. "Okay, maybe it didn't *start* great, but there were some good moments in the middle. We talked, I got her to smile and laugh..." I trail off again, remembering the ethereal sound. I've been aimless for so long, but bringing Sydney joy, even for those brief moments, gave me purpose.

"And then what? What did you do?"

"Maybe it wasn't me that messed up, did you ever think about that?" Grams narrows her eyes, silently calling me out on my bullshit. "Fine, it was me. I panicked and started talking about the hideous new health section at the market."

"For someone as charming and outgoing as you are, you really suck at flirting."

I glare at her. "So I've been told. Anyway, I made a stupid remark about the store hiring an interior designer that was overrated and overpaid."

"Hudson Wolf! Sydney is an interior designer!" Grams looks shocked and horrified. It's almost comical. She's literally clutching her pearls.

"I know that now," I sigh, wiping a hand down my face. "She pretty much sprinted away from me before I got a chance to apologize.

Again." I slump against the bar and rub my temples. "I somehow keep messing up with her. I don't know how to show her I'm not an asshole."

"Keep your mouth shut?" Grams suggests snarkily.

"Ha ha."

"Well, good thing for you, I always have a backup plan or five."

"That doesn't surprise me."

"Hush, boy. Do you want to know where you can find Sydney or not?"

"More stalking then, I see."

"Take it or leave it. I just thought you could use all the help you could get." I nod, more than okay with stalking the goddess, even if it's only to get another glimpse of her. "She's helping Mr. and Mrs. Henderson with the renovation on their old Victorian home. She'll be there all day. Perhaps she could use some help from a certain contrite bartender?"

"I have Brenda coming in for her shift at two. I'll swing by after that."

"That's my Hudson. Don't screw it up this time. It's a lot of work to set up these encounters."

"Something tells me you don't mind snooping and meddling," I tease.

Grams waves her hand at me dismissively, then gets comfortable in one of the booths. The woman may have sold the place to me, but she's still the heart of The Pink Door. She loves being here, even if she's just knitting in the back corner.

The next five hours are excruciatingly slow. Each minute feels like a month, but Brenda finally waltzes in, taking over for me.

The whole way over to the Henderson's, I try to think of what to say to Sydney. Should I apologize right away? Ease myself into a conversation? Watch her from a distance and then chicken out and go home with my tail between my legs?

By the time I pull up next to the old house, I'm no closer to figuring it out than when I started. I hope the words come to me in the moment, but that hasn't exactly worked out in my favor in the past. Still, I have to do something.

The house has been almost completely gutted, with nothing left but the bare bones. Grams told me the Hendersons have been staying with friends while their house is being remodeled. I can see a few construction workers milling about in the yard, as well as a few on the roof. A tarp covers a huge portion of one side of the house, the corner flap blowing up in the breeze.

I see the barest hint of familiar red shoes, shapely legs, and the hem of a pretty blue dress. *Sydney*. My heart thunders in my chest and I swallow down the nerves as I walked toward the tarp.

Ducking inside, I'm greeted with a vision in blue. Sydney's back is facing me, and with all the noise on the roof, she hasn't heard me come in yet. I take a second to appreciate her silhouette, the slight dip in her waist that flows into her wide, mouthwatering hips. And that ass...

This isn't about that, though. I have to earn her trust first.

"Hey," I say over the noise, alerting her to my presence.

Sydney spins around, her eyes wide as she stares at me. For one small second, she almost looks happy to see me. But then she remembers my last words to her, and her eyes drop to the floor.

"Hudson," she murmurs, turning back around and facing the wall she was looking at.

Not a great start, but at least she's not running away. "I heard you were helping the Hendersons with their renovations," I start, risking a step forward.

She nods, then pauses, looking at me over her shoulder. "I'm just a consultant. I'm doing it for free."

"I deserve that," I sigh. I wish she were mad at me, but she just looks sad. I hate putting that look in her eyes. I only ever want her to smile. "Sydney, I feel like a broken record, but I really am sorry. Not only for the misunderstanding the first time we met, but for my careless words at the market."

She nods again but doesn't turn around. Sydney wraps her arms around herself, almost like she needs protection from me. Dammit, this isn't working at all. I think I've just made her more anxious, which was not my intention.

"So, I was thinking I could make it up to you by helping out today."

"No," she says quickly. "That's not necessary."

At first, I think she's dismissing me, but I realize she's nervous. Maybe as nervous as I am.

"I'd really like to help. I promise I'm not the thoughtless jerk you think I am. Not that I blame you. I just can't ever seem to say what I mean."

"And what do you mean?" she asks softly.

I'd like to tell her exactly what I mean. I mean that I'd like to make her mine, claim every inch of her, make her laugh, hold her when she's anxious, and wake up with her every morning. I have to play it safe, though. She's barely talking to me right now, so I don't want to scare her off with declarations of forever.

"For now, just that I'd like to help," I say, instead of spouting off my obsessive thoughts. She finally faces me, tilting her head to the side as she examines me. Her clear green eyes are inquisitive and beyond perceptive. I hope she sees how genuine I am. A small smile tugs at her lips, making me want to beat my chest in victory. "I'm sure you can use a big strong man to do some heavy-lifting, right?" I wink at her and flex, like an idiot. *Why did I say that?*

I know Sydney is thinking the same thing when her smile twists into a scowl. Her green eyes narrow and she balls her fists up, placing them on her hips. As messed up as it is, the spark in her gaze makes me hard.

"I don't need a man to do anything for me, thank you very much," she informs me. Seeing the passion in her eyes, the confidence in her firm voice, and her slightly flushed cheeks has me biting back a groan.

My Sydney may be shy, but she's got a fire deep down inside. It was the same way when I chased her down the street. She was shy, nervous, and yet mouthy. Adorable. *Mine.*

"No, I know that. It was just saying I could make things easier. Faster. You know, help out."

"I don't like taking the easy way out. I'm proud of my work and I want to do things well. You might not appreciate interior design, but it's more than just paint swatches and matching pillows. It's about the flow and balance of a room. It's a feeling, not a formula. Anything less would be shoddy work, and that's not what I do, Hudson."

"Of course not," I say quickly. "I just meant..."

"Why would you want to help anyway? Don't you think interior designers are overrated? If this is about a guilty conscience, don't worry about it."

"But I *am* worried about it. And I don't think interior designers are overrated," I insist.

Sydney turns back around, facing the wall. I hate that she's trembling. I somehow know it's from both anger and anxiety. Fuck me, I made her feel both of those things.

I'm losing her, and fast. I need a way to be around her again.

"In fact, I'm in the market for one myself." *What am I doing?* She half turns, eyeing me over her shoulder again. "Yeah. I recently took over The Pink Door from my grandma. Connie Wolf. You might know her as the town gossip?" I go for a joke, and even though she doesn't want to, Sydney's lips twitch into the barest hint of a smile. "It's a little outdated and I'd love some fresh eyes on the place. I may not know the first thing about design, and certainly not enough for me to make that horrible comment at the market. But I do appreciate what you and those in your profession do. Like you said, I know there are behind-the-scenes things that go on that would confuse the fuck out of me, I'm sure." Her cheeks glow with a blush, and she nibbles on her bottom lip as she turns to face me. I hope that's a good sign. "So, would you consider taking a look at the place? I'll pay you, of course."

Sydney perks up at that. I'm sure she needs some real-world experience if she's applying for jobs right out of college. Having this house remodel and the bar remodel on her resume is a good start.

I take a step closer to her and resist the urge to pull her into my arms. She has to tilt her head almost all the way back to meet my gaze. Her petite frame covered in lush curves is almost more than I can take, but I manage to stay focused.

"Please?" I ask softly. "I keep making a fool out of myself in front of you, but all I want is to get to know you."

Sydney blinks up at me, then rubs her lips together. She looks deep in thought, and I wonder if that's a habit of hers when mulling over a decision. I want to know all of her habits and quirks, but first, I need her to see I'm not a monster.

She's about to say yes. I know it. I risk brushing my fingers against hers, then holding her hand. Sydney gasps, and I know she felt it. That spark of attraction, the undeniable pull we have toward each other.

Sydney squeezes my hand and then steps back, breaking our connection. "I don't think that's a good idea, Hudson. Thanks for thinking of me though."

Before I can get another word out, my future wife ducks around me and escapes through the tarp wall.

"Dammit," I sigh, running my fingers through my hair. This is the third time she's run away from me, and I'm praying it will be the last. I don't know what the next step is, I just know I'm not giving up.

Chapter Six

Sydney

"You're up early," my grandma says, joining me at the kitchen table with a cup of coffee.

"I didn't sleep much last night," I admit.

"Are you not feeling well?" She reaches out and presses the back of her hand on my forehead, checking for a temperature.

"I'm not sick or anything," I assure her. "I just..." I let out an exasperated sigh. I've always told my grandmother everything. It might make me sound lame, but she's just as much my best friend as Evangeline and Rowan.

"Tell me what's on your mind, dear. Are you worried about finding a job? You know I love having you back here in Cherry Falls and you're welcome to stay with me for however long it takes. I know you're working your hardest and I'm sure something will come your way soon."

"Thanks, Grandma," I say with a smile, squeezing her hand. She really is the most supportive person in the world. "I actually sort of was offered a job yesterday."

"What? That's so exciting! Why do you look so anxious about it?"

I laugh and roll my eyes. "I mean, that's kind of my thing, right? Freaking out over changes and the unknown," I joke.

"Don't talk about yourself that way. You've been through a hell of a lot more than most people your age and you've done an amazing job at growing, healing, and becoming a wonderful young woman."

"I have you to thank for that, you know."

"You're right. I do good work, huh?" she says with a wink. "Now tell me what's really going on."

I take a sip of coffee, prolonging the inevitable. "Hudson Wolf came to see me yesterday at the Henderson's house."

"He did?!" my grandma exclaims, perking up right away. "I mean, that's interesting," she quickly recovers. Weird.

"Yeah..." I narrow my eyes at her, but she just smiles sweetly. "Anyway, he asked if I would come look at The Pink Door and give ideas for a remodel and decorations to bring it into the modern age."

"How wonderful!" The old woman is practically swooning. She seems far too invested in this, but I'm not sure why. Maybe she's just happy to get me out of the house for a bit.

"Well, the thing is, Hudson is kind of an arrogant jerk."

"That doesn't sound like the Hudson I know. You had that little misunderstanding about the shepherd's pie, but that was cleared up, right?"

"No! Not at all! I still have no idea what upset him so much. And then I saw him at the Rosewood Market, where he proceeded to tell me interior designers are overpaid and overrated." Grandma's eyes go wide, but I continue. "Then, yesterday, he waltzes into the Henderson's place, acting like he was there to save the day and help me do all the heavy lifting because he's a big strong man. I don't know, it all just rubbed me the wrong way."

"I think the man is tongue-tied when he's around you, dear."

I consider her words but dismiss them right away. "No, that's impossible." Though, he has said several times that he just wants to spend time with me and get to know me. But why? I mean, he's a freaking Greek god with dark hair and mesmerizing eyes. Not to mention, he's older, established, and has his life figured out. Why would he be interested in a big girl with anxiety and baggage?

"Why would you say that?"

"I mean, come on." I gesture around my face and body.

"Sydney Danielle Reese. If you're implying you're not pretty or good enough for Hudson, or anyone, for that matter, I haven't raised you right." I don't say anything, because there's nothing to say. She doesn't tolerate negative self-talk, and I should have known better.

"Anyway. That's a conversation for another time. Hudson aside, why are you hesitant to take the job? It'd be great experience and I'm sure Hudson is going to pay you."

I nod, choosing my words carefully. "Honestly, I think... I'm afraid to take the lead on a project. I mean, I've never been in charge of a project for a real place. What if he hates it? What if I waste his money on something hideous? What if I order ten thousand tiles of the wrong shape or color and it all falls apart and the bar goes out of business and it's all my fault?"

I let out a huge breath after my little meltdown and then gulp down the rest of my coffee to keep from rambling on even more. Unfortunately, the caffeine only accelerates my spiral.

"First of all, Sydney, you're not going to screw up so badly that The Pink Door will shut down. It's in an institution around here," she says in a calming voice. "But also, these are the kinds of things you have to work through. You can't run from it. And the way I see it, even if you don't like working with Hudson, that will give you some good experience, too. You'll have other difficult clients in the future, so it will be good practice on how to handle them. Or, maybe Hudson will surprise you by being a gentleman. Who knows, maybe this will be the start of something amazing."

"You seem to have a very high opinion of someone who has insulted me several times now," I reply, narrowing my eyes at her.

"Don't take my word for it. Go have a chat with him and see what he's offering and what kinds of projects he wants to be done. What's the harm in getting some more information?"

Approximately seven hundred and sixty-two ways it could cause harm and go terribly awry cross my mind, but I shove them way down deep and take a calming breath. Grandma is right. I need to step up and make some career-defining choices, starting with The Pink Door. This is about getting experience, and nothing else. Hudson will have to chill out eventually, right?

"You're right," I admit.

"I know." I laugh and Grandma smiles and pats my cheek. "I bet Hudson will be at the bar in an hour or so. You can catch him before he gets too busy with other projects."

Once again, I examine my grandmother. She seems awfully keen on getting me together with Hudson. I brush that thought aside. It doesn't matter what her motivation is. I need to make this choice for myself. I just hope I chose wisely.

An hour and a half later, I'm standing in front of The Pink Door. Literally. I'm staring at the namesake hot pink door, trying to calm my nerves. I've already wiped my hands on my dress so many times the fabric is damp, but my palms are still clammy.

A shiver runs down my spine, and I rub my lips together before blowing out a breath. *I can do this. Just walk in and talk to him. No big deal.*

Despite my nerves, I manage a hollow laugh. It's a very big deal. I can't lie about that. Nevertheless, I have to try. My grandma's words come back to me from our conversation the other day. *Choose your future based on your hopes, not your fears.*

Squaring my shoulders, I lift a trembling hand to the door and pull it open, stepping inside the dimly lit bar.

Thankfully, I don't see Hudson. In fact, I don't see anyone. The place isn't open yet, and I assume Hudson is in the back. In any other town, it would be foolish to leave this door unlocked outside of operating hours, but Rosewood is one of those places where hardly anyone locks up. It's a safe community, and almost too picture-perfect to be real.

I take the opportunity to check out the place on my own, without anyone hovering over my shoulder. The bar is eclectic, with a mix of dark wood furniture, a gorgeous oak bar top, and an assortment of gold and silver light fixtures adorning the walls in even intervals. There's a dance floor with a jukebox and a chandelier instead of a disco ball. Surprisingly, there aren't any other pink accents, just the front door.

Stepping closer to one of the walls, I notice the damask pattern isn't painted on like I originally thought. It's wallpaper.

"What are you doing here?"

Hudson's voice startles me, and with my nerves already frayed, I jump backward and make a horrid banshee-screeching noise.

"Shit," Hudson hisses, his arms immediately surrounding me so I don't fall over. "I don't think I'm ever going to make a good impression, am I?"

I look up into those stupidly gorgeous blue eyes. I lose track of time as I count the different shades of blue. They would make an amazing color palette for a calming ambiance.

And then he smiles.

Good freaking God, he has dimples. And full lips. And white teeth that I suddenly want to feel sinking into my skin.

What the heck?

"Fourth time's the charm?" I whisper, unable to look away from him.

Hudson is still holding me close. My hands are pressed against his firm chest while he secures me with a hand on my waist and one on my back. The man's eyes sparkle as his smile spreads, and holy crap, he's somehow beautiful, masculine, comforting, and commanding all at once.

"Damn, is this really the fourth time I've messed up with you?"

"Who's counting?" I've never flirted before. Is that what's happening? Is that what I want to happen? My brain is scrambled from being this close to him. It doesn't help that he smells like peppermint and pine needles. I want to bottle it up and spray it all over my sheets.

"I am," he says, his voice turning somber. "You've got me all out of sorts, Sydney." His voice is soft and warm, and he starts gently caressing my back. Amazingly, each stroke up and down my spine calms me down.

"Me?" I squeak out.

Hudson grins and cups the side of my face with his other hand. I lean into his touch, powerless to do anything but soak up his attention. "You, sweet girl. It's cliché as fuck, but I've never felt this connection with anyone. I know I'm horrible at flirting, as evidenced by the incident at the market, and further proved by my idiocy yesterday at the Henderson's."

"I make you... nervous?" My grandma said the same thing and Evan mentioned it at the cafe that day as well. The idea of little ol' me making anyone nervous is laughable, let alone someone who looks and smiles like Hudson.

He nods his head, then drops his hand from my face, circling his fingers around my wrist instead. He moves my hand so it's resting right over his heart. "Feel how fast it's beating? This is what you do to me. Knowing I've hurt you has been the worst kind of torture, and knowing it's happened multiple times? Makes me sick to my stomach. I can't sleep at night. Fuck, I'm coming on too strong."

I don't realize I'm gaping at him until he takes a step back. I sway toward him, already missing his warmth. "No. I mean, maybe. It's kind of crazy. But I can tell you're being genuine." Hudson nods and I look down at my balled-up hands, trying to let go of the tension. Slowly, I relax my fingers, uncurling them enough so my nails aren't digging into my palms. "I still don't know what happened earlier. You were nice and then angry and then chased me down. You seemed nice again at the market, but then..." I trail off, shrugging. "And yesterday, I may have gone overboard with reprimanding you, but—"

"Never apologize to me, Sydney." Hudson steps closer, cupping my face in his hands once more. I love it. I crave it. I had no idea how much I would like being handled this way, and by the hottest man I've ever seen, for that matter. "I deserved every word. I swear I'm not that guy. As for the first day we met... well, I think you need to ask your grandmother about that one."

I raise an eyebrow at him, but he doesn't give me any more information. I have a feeling our meddling grandmothers had something to do with the setup, but that still doesn't excuse his behavior.

Hudson strokes his thumbs back and forth over my cheeks, the light touch making me sensitive everywhere.

"As for the stupid remark at the store..." he sighs and dips his head down, dropping his hands from my face. I miss his touch, but not for long. His hands land on my hips, anchoring me in place. An unbearable pressure pulses from my core, making me squeeze my thighs together. "I was trying to ask you out for coffee."

A laugh escapes my lips, but I quickly cover my mouth with my hand. Hudson looks sheepish, the tips of his ears burning bright red. This man is blushing. Because of me.

"I know, I know, it was a horrible strategy," he continues, though he seems lighter now that I'm laughing. "You're just so fucking beautiful and sweet and I've never been so flustered."

"Really?" Me? Beautiful?

"You have to know how stunning you are. And knowing you're talented and so damn kind as well... you're kind of the whole package, Sydney."

"Wow," I breathe out, my eyes never leaving his. Hudson reaches out and tucks some of my hair behind my ear. I see his eyes dart to the scar on my forehead, and I instinctively tip my head down, letting my long bangs cover it up.

Hudson gently cups my chin and guides my head up so we're face to face once more. "Beautiful," he whispers, brushing my bangs out of the way once more. "Precious," he says, right before pressing his lips to my scar.

I fight back tears at his words, spoken so reverently as he handles me with such care.

I don't know how long we stay like that, with Hudson cradling me while he nuzzles into the top of my head, but it's still too soon when he steps away from me. His hand finds mine, and Hudson tugs me along toward a booth in the back.

"Now, tell me why you're here, Sydney. As much as I'd love it to be to visit me, I get the sense there's something else."

"I was reconsidering your offer, that is if it's still on the table."

"Hell yes!" he exclaims. "I mean, yes. Of course," he says in a more normal voice.

I try, unsuccessfully, to hide a smile at his eagerness. It's a nice little confidence booster. It wasn't just guilt that drove Hudson to ask me to work on his bar. He's sincerely happy to be around me, just like he's told me several times already.

"Good. So, this is my first big project," I say tentatively. I would understand if he wants someone with more experience, so I want to be honest about it. "But I think I can help spruce this place up. Some new fixtures, different colors, and updated lighting will make a world of difference. And then there's the wallpaper..." I trail off, my eyes wandering over to one of the walls.

My nose is scrunched up, and when I look back at Hudson, he's grinning at me like he thinks I'm adorable. It's a new feeling, but I don't hate it. In fact, I think I very much like it.

"That bad, huh?"

"It's... not great. But I'm mostly just thinking about how much work it's going to be to strip it off."

"We can't just paint over it?"

My jaw drops and my eyes nearly bug out of my head. "No!" I gasp, horrified that he would suggest that.

Hudson chuckles and reaches across the table, taking my hand in his. "See? You're perfect. I would have painted over everything and ruined it. You're already saving this place from total destruction on day one."

I blush at his compliment but wave him off. "I haven't done anything yet. But I'd like to come up with a plan of attack tomorrow. That is if you're ready to start that soon."

"Yes, yes, yes, a million times yes!"

I grin at his playfulness. He's being so kind and charming. Maybe he really was nervous to be around me. That gives me the confidence to move forward with the renovation. Maybe Grandma was right this morning. Maybe this will be the start of something amazing.

Chapter Seven

Hudson

I check my watch for the tenth time this morning. It's only eight-fifteen, but I've been up for hours. Today is Sydney's first day on the job, and I want everything to be perfect.

I got an assortment of pastries for breakfast, as well as a nice flower arrangement from The Garden Goddess. The owner, Evangeline, gave me a curious look when ringing up my order, but then she winked at me and said she approved. I know she's close with my Sydney, so I hope this means I'll have some support when it comes to wooing my sweet girl.

Sydney is supposed to be here at eight-thirty, so I do one final check to make sure everything is in place. The scones, muffins, donuts, and croissants are arranged on a platter, and the colorful flower arrangement is right next to it. I have a glass for water and a cup for coffee, both of which I'll fill when she gets here to make sure it's fresh.

I'm not sure what changed between the last time I saw her and the Henderson home and when she came into the bar yesterday, but I'm not about to question it. For some reason, Sydney decided to give me a fourth chance to make a good impression. I will *not* screw it up this time.

I need Sydney in a profound, almost unbearable way. Especially now that I know how soft her skin is and how her breath sounds when I whisper sweet words to her. My lips still burn from where I kissed her forehead as if she branded me with that one touch. I hated that she tried to hide her scar from me. I'll figure out what happened soon enough, but I needed her to know she's perfect. Flawless. Everything about her calls out to me.

The front door cracks open, letting in a beam of light from the outside. There, standing in the entrance, is my queen, her curves silhouetted by the sun streaming in behind her. It's all I can do to keep from growling at the sight of her.

"Am I too early?" the ethereal beauty asks me, jarring me from my thoughts.

"No, you're perfect," I tell her, grinning from ear to ear. I probably look like a crazy person, but Sydney doesn't seem to mind. She even rewards me with a soft smile and the hint of a blush on her adorable, round cheeks.

"Oh my gosh, what is all of this? Is there a crew of people showing up to help or something?"

"No, just you and me for now, sweetheart." Sydney's blush turns crimson, and hell yes, I see the way she's squeezing her thighs together as she stands in front of me, looking over the breakfast spread out on the bar top. "I didn't know what you liked, so I got a bit of everything."

"Wow," she murmurs. "You didn't have to do all that for me."

"But I want to," I assure her. "Plus, I need my interior designer to be well taken care of so she can work her magic in here."

"Right," she says with a nod. Sydney twists her fingers together nervously before shaking her hands out. I can tell she's trying to get rid of her nerves, and I hate that she's still anxious around me.

"Come on, let's dig in, and then we can talk about your ideas. We're just in the planning phase right now."

My words seem to have their intended effect, and I watch Sydney relax her shoulders and take a deep breath. Soon, my sweet girl will know she never has to be shy or nervous around me. Until then, I'll do everything in my power to calm her fears.

I turn around and grab the coffee pot, giving her a chance to sit down and get comfortable without me staring at her. When I face her again, I almost drop the coffee on the floor. She's just that damn beautiful, perched on a barstool, leaning over my bar, and giving me a shy little smile.

"How do you take your coffee, sweetheart?" Sydney's smile grows wider at my endearment. That has to be a good sign, right?

"Half coffee, half cream and sugar," she says with a little laugh.

"Coming right up." I pour the coffee into her mug and then set out the creamer and a bowl of sugar packets.

Sydney seems reluctant to try the food, so I dig right in, grabbing a donut, a bagel, and a muffin. I know some girls don't like eating in front of guys, but I don't want her to ever feel ashamed of that stuff around me. It pisses me off that our culture has dictated that women should be a certain size and pretend to eat only salads. It's as unrealistic as it is sexist.

My girl looks at my plate and grins, finally reaching out for a donut and a muffin. I grunt, satisfied to feed my woman and provide for her in this way. Sydney glances over at me, probably wondering what that sound was. I smile and give her a wink before shoving half of a blueberry muffin in my mouth. Crumbs scatter all over my shirt, the bar, and the floor, but Sydney's tinkling laughter is worth it. I'll look like a fool for her anytime, as long as she's smiling.

Sydney takes a bite of her chocolate frosted donut, letting out a breathy moan as she swallows. Jesus fucking Christ, it's not even fair how sexy she is. And she has no idea. I can't wait to show her when the time is right.

She looks over at me, her cheeks back to that soft pink I love so much. Sydney has a bit of frosting on her lip, and without thinking, I wipe it off with my thumb. At first, she freezes. But then she surprises the fuck out of me by licking it off.

Goddamn. My dick springs to life, pressing painfully against my metal zipper.

"Oh my gosh," Sydney gasps. "I don't know what I was thinking. That was so unprofessional and... and..."

"I loved it," I growl, cutting her off. "Never apologize for putting your lips on me."

She rubs her lips together in that nervous gesture of hers, and I take another risk by cupping her face. My thumb rubs against her mouth gently, coaxing her to release her pouty pink lips once more.

"That's better," I murmur, swiping my thumb over her bottom lip and pulling it down slightly. Her green eyes flash with heat and lust, and it takes everything in me to pull back instead of crash my lips over hers and take her right here on the bar.

We finish our breakfast, making small talk here and there. Sydney isn't completely comfortable around me yet, but I think I've made a lot of good progress this morning. I'm hoping to get even closer as we work together today.

"Ready to discuss your ideas?" I ask once I've cleared everything away and stored the leftovers in a bag for her to take home.

"Yeah, sure," she says, her voice a little higher than usual. She rummages around in the giant purse she brought, pulling out a portfolio with sketches and notes. "This is my first big project, so I don't want you to get your hopes up. And these ideas are really rough. The sketches are just drafts."

"Hey," I say softly, sitting down next to her at the bar. "Don't sell yourself short. You don't have to preface your designs or take away from the hard work you've already done."

Sydney eyes me warily like she doesn't quite believe me. Still, she opens the portfolio and takes out a few sketches, placing them on the table in front of us.

I'm truly stunned. Not only are the sketches masterfully drawn, but she managed to keep the eclectic feeling my grams loves so much while still cleaning up the look and modernizing a few things.

The details and thoughts that went into these sketches are astounding. Did she really do all of this in one night? How is that possible?

"Like I said, they are really rough..."

"Sydney, these are incredible," I tell her honestly. "How did you have time to do all of this?"

"Unemployed, remember?" she says with a little smirk, pointing to herself.

"Seriously, sweetheart. These must have taken hours, let alone the time spent researching and coming up with the ideas."

"It was a late night, but it was worth it." She sips the last of her coffee before setting it down and focusing her attention on me. For the first time, I see she has dark circles under her eyes. My poor girl is exhausted. She must have really been nervous about this project if she lost sleep over it.

"I appreciate your dedication, but I don't want to burn you out. You need your beauty rest." As soon as the words are out of my mouth, I realize how that might have come across. "I didn't mean—"

Sydney laughs, making my stress melt away. "I know what you mean, I just like seeing you squirm."

I chuckle and comb my fingers through my hair, delighted that she's teasing me. "Cruel, but fair," I say with a grin. "So, tell me about your plan. Where do we start? What do you need?"

Sydney looks over her portfolio with a renewed passion. She's excited to talk about what she came up with, and I eat up every word. Now that she's over the initial anxiety, Sydney gains some of her confidence back.

She points out the light fixtures that need to be replaced, booths and stools that need to be reupholstered, and a more intuitive way to arrange the tables to avoid congestion from the bar to the dance floor.

"This is far above what I thought you'd do," I say in awe.

"Oh. I'm sorry, I just got excited I guess."

"What? No, I meant that as a good thing. You're incredible and I'm amazed by you."

"Are you Hudson's twin?" she asks, half-jokingly.

"You mean because I'm not being a jerk for once?" She grins, and I smile right back. I love that we're mostly past the damage I've done with my careless words and actions. "Sorry to disappoint, but it's still me, through and through."

"Shame." It comes out a little too stilted to be smooth, but I love that even more. She's flirting with me. I can tell she's not used to it, and neither am I. Truthfully, I'm glad. I don't like the thought of her flirting with other men or giving them any attention whatsoever.

Sydney hops off the stool and wanders over to the nearest wall, examining the wallpaper. I walk up next to her, observing as she picks at one of the curled-up edges. Her cute little nose is scrunched up, just like it was yesterday.

"That bad, huh?" I ask.

"It'll be fine. I mean, it'll be a pain in the ass, but I think we can do it. We'll need some dissolvent for the glue and a lot of elbow grease, but it's definitely doable."

I hum and nod my head, already thinking about who I can ask for help. There's no way I'm letting Sydney tire herself out by ripping down wallpaper. She must take my silence as disapproval, however.

"Or we can leave it," she says quickly. "Like I said, this is my first big project, and to be honest, the first one I've ever taken a lead on. There are a lot of things I still don't know. Some people might like hideous wallpaper. Shoot, I mean, not that it's *hideous*, per se. It's just—"

"Hideous is an excellent word for it," I say, not wanting her to doubt herself for a single second longer. She tends to talk really fast when she's anxious, something I picked up on while I was trying to make a good impression. "And just because you've never taken the lead on a project doesn't mean you don't have intuition and talent. I can see both of those things in your sketches, and I can't wait to see your vision come to life."

Sydney looks up at me, her eyes shining with tears. Fuck, what did I say this time?

Before I realize what's happening, Sydney wraps her arms around me, squeezing me in the warmest hug I've ever had. I fold her into my embrace and my hand cups the back of her neck, massaging the clenched muscles there. My poor girl is so tense. Her muscles must be aching from all the anxiety she carries in them.

Gently weaving my fingers through her hair, I tug slightly, so she's looking up at me. I kiss her forehead and temple, leaning down to brush my lips against the shell of her ear. I don't know where the words come from, but something tells me she needs to hear them.

"You're so talented, sweet girl. And I'm not just saying that because I'm smitten with you." Sydney shivers and then lets out a breathy little laugh. I smile, kissing her temple again. "I'm proud of you for showing up today. I get the sense it was really difficult, but thank you for trusting me."

Sydney nods her head, which is buried against my chest. I tighten my hold on her hair, pulling lightly to angle her face toward mine. I give her time to push me away or escape my embrace, but instead, she sways ever closer to me, until our mouths are inches apart. Her breath tickles my skin, her lips slightly parted, so soft and welcoming.

"I'm going to kiss you now, my sweet Sydney."

She nods her head, giving me all the permission I need.

My mouth hovers above her for one last second, savoring this moment. Nothing will be the same once I taste her sweetness.

Our lips brush together softly, and then I pull her closer, sealing my mouth over hers.

My heart squeezes up tightly and then thuds against my chest, releasing a rush of endorphins and adrenaline. She's so damn sweet, so responsive, so soft and welcoming. I part her lips with my tongue, slowly stroking it against hers until a quiet, needy moan escapes her mouth.

I swallow it down and take a few steps forward, backing her into the wall and pressing her against it. "You're perfect," I whisper before claiming her once again.

My hands wander down her body, pausing to appreciate her curves. Sydney rolls her hips, brushing against my raging hard cock. She gasps, and I try angling myself away from her, worried that it's too much.

When she whimpers and rubs herself against me even harder, I go fucking crazy.

My hands cup her ass and I knead her soft flesh, pulling her closer and helping her grind against me. Sydney shivers and tips her head back, catching her breath. I continue kissing and nipping her neck, finding all the spots that make her writhe in pleasure.

"Hudson," she murmurs, sliding her hands up my chest and wrapping them around my neck.

"Sydney," I growl, lifting her up in my arms and pinning her against the wall with my body.

I dive right back in, deepening our kiss, stroking my tongue in and out of her hot, wet little mouth while pumping my hips against her sweet heat. Christ, I can feel her arousal through her dress, her needy pussy begging me to take care of it.

My girl digs her nails into the back of my neck, using me as leverage to grind herself against my thick, aching dick. I dry fuck her into the wall, knowing it's too much, too soon, but unable to stop. Especially when she keeps moaning my name.

"I've got you," I whisper, resting my cheek against hers. I feel her choppy, uneven breaths against my ear, each one more ragged and desperate than the last until she sounds absolutely possessed.

Fucking hell, she's a needy little thing. I love it. I'll always satisfy her, whenever she asks me to.

"Do you want to come for me, sweetheart?"

"I-I-I don't know if-f-f I can," she admits. Her body is sending me the exact opposite signals.

"You can. I need it. Need to hold you when it hits you, when it drags you under, and when it leaves you limp and sated."

"Oh, God," she moans. "Hudson... I... oh, God, it feels..."

"How does it feel?" I grunt, dipping my head to lick a bead of sweat off her neck.

"L-l-like I'm on fire e-everywhere and something... Oh, God, some-something is happening..."

"Fuck," I groan, grinding down on her while slipping my tongue between her lips. Each time my jean-covered cock scrapes against her center, Sydney gasps and lets out a wanton little moan, encouraging me to continue. "Let go, Sydney. Let it happen. Let me see you come apart for me."

She squeezes her eyes shut and clamps her thighs around me, every muscle in her body strung so damn tight. And then she snaps, unraveling in my arms as her pleasure pulses through her.

Sydney opens her mouth in a silent scream, and I bury my face between her neck and shoulder, pumping into her with rough, shallow strokes, prolonging her orgasm until she's limp in my arms.

I gently set her back down on the ground, and then wrap my arms around her, pressing kisses to the top of her head.

"Holy cow," comes the muffled response of my sweet girl.

"Yeah," I chuckle, rocking her back and forth. This feels so fucking right. She has to feel it, too, right? I take a chance, admittedly, hoping the orgasm softened her up a bit. "Go out with me."

Sydney giggles, then peers up at me, those green eyes hitting me square in the chest. "Want to try again?" she asks, a playful sparkle in her eyes.

"Sydney Reese, will you do me the honor of accompanying me for dinner at a date and time of your choosing?"

She giggles again, the light sound filling me up. "Dial it back a bit."

"Sydney, my beautiful girl. I'd love to spend an evening getting to know you more. Will you let me take you out?"

Her face turns more serious as she considers my question. "Yeah, I think I'd like that."

"Fuck yes," I grunt right before slanting my mouth over hers. I can't help it. I want to taste those words on my tongue.

When we break apart, Sydney gives me a bright smile, her eyes still shining with lust. It's my new favorite look of hers.

Chapter Eight

Sydney

"What are you wearing?" Evan asks via our three-way FaceTime call with Rowan.

"Oh! Try on that red maxi dress!" Rowan says while rocking Harper on her hip.

"Yeah! With your wedge heels. The ones Rowan made you get that I know you've never worn."

"I stand by that recommendation, by the way," Rowan says flatly, making Evan laugh.

"Yes to the red dress, no to the shoes," I finally say, reaching for the dress in the back of my closet. "It's the first date. I don't want to fall on my butt and make a fool out of myself."

"Actually, that might be perfect," Rowan says. "I mean, Hudson has already embarrassed himself in front of you like a million times. Maybe you even the playing field a bit."

Evan laughs, and I join her. I called my besties as soon as I got home from The Pink Door yesterday. They've been dying for an update ever since I told them I officially accepted his job offer.

I should have probably played it cool when Hudson asked me out, but everything about that moment was overwhelming in the best way. I was still coming down from the most intense experience of my life with my heart racing, my cheeks flushed, and my lips still wet and swollen from his kiss. I could hardly stand up let alone refuse the man who had just turned my world upside down.

"Earth to Sydney!" Evan calls out.

"I think we lost her," Rowan replies.

"I'm here, I'm here," I say with a laugh. "Okay, the red dress is a yes, but I'm thinking of the black strappy sandals instead of wedges. At least the sandals are flat."

"Fine," Rowan sighs dramatically.

"You'll look great no matter what," Evan follows up, giving me a smile through the screen.

"You know I'm just kidding," Rowan says. "I mean, I do want to see you in those gorgeous wedges before they go out of style, but the most important thing is for you to feel confident about tonight."

"Ha, yeah, right," I mutter. "This is so far outside my comfort zone! Why did I agree to this? What if he realizes he actually hates me and then I'm out a job and a hot bar owner? What if I sneeze with a mouthful of food and it sprays all over him? What if—"

"Okay, I'm going to have to cut you off there," Evan says. I nod my head and rub my lips together. I always ramble nervously when I'm anxious and feel out of control. "Listen to me, Syd. Hudson is truly a nice guy and an upstanding citizen by all accounts. He was a Marine, he loves his grandma, and so far, he seems to be a great business owner. I mean, he hired you after all."

Rowan nods her head, agreeing with Evan. "And, look at it this way. Even if, on the slight chance, you happen to do something you think is embarrassing, just think about the times Hudson called you a liar, insulted your profession, and then said you needed a big strong man to do your work for you."

"That's not exactly how it happened," I say, coming to his defense.

"*And*," Evan interrupts, "I thought we were trying to *encourage* Sydney to go on the date, not remind her of all the other stuff he's done."

"Oh, I still very much approve of the date," Rowan says, nodding her head. "I'm just saying, if anyone could understand getting tongue-tied or saying something wrong, it's Hudson. So take a breath and trust that he's just as nervous as you right now."

Huh. I hadn't thought of it that way before. "Thanks, guys. This was actually really helpful."

"You sound surprised," Evan teases.

"Whatever, you know I love you."

"Love you, too!" she answers.

"Love ya, Syd. We'll let you finish getting ready," Rowan says.

Fifteen minutes later, I'm in the red maxi dress and strappy sandals, waiting anxiously for Hudson to show up. I left my hair down, letting the naturally wavy locks fall down my back and over one shoulder.

I considered putting on makeup, but it felt fake. I hardly ever wear anything other than a light concealer and maybe some lip gloss if I'm feeling fancy. After watching ten YouTube tutorials on how to get the perfect smokey eye and shaping your eyebrows, I gave up. That's not who I am, and that's not who Hudson asked out.

A smile spreads across my face whenever I think about it. He's kind of adorable, which is a far cry from the Hudson I met the first day. Rowan is right. I seem to make Hudson nervous, though I can't understand why.

A knock on the door rattles me out of my thoughts. Heat flashes through my body, followed by a chill that makes me shiver and turns my hands clammy. He's here.

Taking one last calming breath, I gather up my purse and open the door with a trembling hand. Hudson grins at me, his blue eyes shining with excitement. Did I put that look on his face? Hudson is wearing a navy blue Henley, stretched across his expansive chest. The shirt clings to his rounded arms, highlighting the contours of each muscle.

My eyes dip lower, though I know it's indecent. I can't seem to help myself, though. His jeans are dark and fit him like they were made just for his thick thighs. I can see the outline of a slight bulge, and a blush spreads across my face. I rub my lips together, remembering what it felt like to rub myself wantonly against his body, feeling his thickness grind against my core until...

"Damn, Sydney," Hudson growls. "You look incredible." I let out a tiny gasp when his subtle erection twitches and grows in length right before my eyes. "Can't look at me like that, sweetheart," he groans.

My eyes snap up to his, and what I see there floors me. He looks absolutely ravenous, hungry for me. There's also a tenderness there like he knows I'm not quite ready for all of him yet.

When Hudson smiles and cups my cheek, I know I'm dangerously close to falling for him. And when he leans in, brushing his lips against mine in the sweetest kiss, I know I can trust him to be all of my firsts.

"Let's get out of here, beautiful," he whispers, lacing his fingers in mine and guiding me outside to his car.

The ride to Hudson's place is quiet but in a comfortable way. I like that he doesn't need to fill the silence. I don't feel pressure to make small talk, especially when he reaches over the console and wraps his hand around mine. He truly does seem content to be in my presence. I don't know much about Hudson yet, but I know it was worth giving him another chance.

He must be thinking the same thing. Hudson squeezes my hand and pulls into the parking lot of The Pink Door, stopping in front of the back entrance before shutting off the car and turning to face me. "Thank you for coming here tonight," he says. "I was going to take you out somewhere fancy because you deserve every good and wonderful thing, but then I thought a low-key night might be better." He stares down at our entwined hands and then peers up at me. "Unless you want to go out. I can—"

"This is perfect," I tell him truthfully. We've both spent enough time miscommunicating that I want to be clear and let him know he doesn't have to be so nervous. "Honestly, I was feeling anxious about tonight, so dinner at your place sounds great." He looks so relieved that I give him another piece of me. "I get pretty anxious in crowds," I confess. "Sometimes I feel like I can't filter anything. It's like every light is too bright and shining right on me, and any slight noise is amplified times a thousand. I get sensory overload and can't process stuff, and... well, anyway, I'm easier to handle alone and in small doses," I joke.

"Thank you for telling me more about you," Hudson says softly. "I promise I can handle anything that comes our way, sweet girl. And I don't want you in small doses. In fact, I think I'll need some extended exposure to you from now on. You've already got me addicted, Sydney."

I'm not sure what to say to that, so I just smile and look down at our hands as a blush burns across my face.

"Anyway," Hudson says, clearing his throat. "Let's get you inside. I've got dinner warming up in the oven. Chicken and roasted potatoes and veggies sound good?"

"I was hoping for the shepherd's pie, but..."

Hudson pulls on my hand, making me fall into him over the console. His lips meet mine once, twice, three times, and then he cups the back of my neck and slides his tongue inside my mouth, kissing me with such intensity I can't do anything but breathe him in and surrender.

"I like seeing your feisty side, beautiful," he murmurs, kissing the tip of my nose before getting out of the car.

He leads me up the stairs to his apartment above The Pink Door with a hand at the small of my back. Once inside, Hudson closes the door and crowds me against it, his entire body pressing against mine and making me squirm.

"Hudson," I breathe out, sliding my hands up his chest. He tips his head back and groans at my touch, encouraging me to wrap my arms around his neck.

"God, Sydney, you're too damn tempting for your own good," he murmurs, his voice low as he rolls his hips against mine. A breathy moan leaves my lips when his thickness rubs against my stomach. "Gonna kiss you now, precious."

I hardly have time to register his new endearment for me before his hand is in my hair, angling me just right for him to kiss the air from my lungs. Hudson wraps his other arm around my waist, holding me against him tightly as if he'll never get enough.

When we finally break apart, I'm breathless and panting.

A timer goes off, causing Hudson to curse under his breath. I grin at him, especially when he starts pouting. God, this man.

I wander around the apartment while he finishes getting dinner ready. I notice how organized and clean everything is. The coffee table shines as if he just cleaned it before I got here. The hardwood floors glow under the soft light of a lamp on one of the side tables. There's a big area rug in the living room that has been purchased recently. I see the tag sticking out on one side, and smile to myself. Did he scrub his apartment clean and then go out and buy a rug for tonight?

I double-check that Hudson is still busy in the kitchen, then kneel down and tuck the tag under the rug. I have a feeling he'd be embarrassed if I knew how much trouble he went to for this date, though he has no need to be. It's incredibly sweet. It also shows me everyone must be right about Hudson. He's a good guy, he just needs to relax. If anyone can understand that, it's me.

"Dinner is served!" Hudson announces. I make my way to the table right as he sets down our plates.

"Oh my gosh, Hudson, this looks delicious!" He has a feast spread out for us. My mouth waters at the sight of it.

"Agreed," he grunts, causing me to look over at him. He's eyeing me, not the food. I roll my eyes at him, but I know my blush is back in full force. I'm not sure what to do with all of his attention. "Sorry," Hudson says while shaking his head. "I know I'm coming on strong."

"It's okay," I whisper, taking his hand. "I don't mind." The smile that spreads across his handsome face is enough to make my belly flop and my heart riot inside my chest.

Once seated, we dig into our food, which of course, is incredible. He asks me a bit about my grandma and college. I can tell he wants to ask about the scar on my forehead, but he doesn't bring it up. It's not that I don't want to tell him, but it's not exactly first-date chit-chat. I appreciate the way he's letting me steer the conversation while still contributing and making me feel like my opinion matters. Hudson hangs on my every word, seemingly thankful for each one I speak.

"So, I heard you were in the Marines before taking over The Pink Door?" I ask after finishing up my last bite.

Hudson nods as he pushes his empty plate back. "Yeah, I was in for twelve years. Did two tours overseas and then moved around to a few different bases."

"Thank you for your service." The words feel inadequate and cliché, but Hudson just smiles as he scoots his chair closer to mine, taking my hand in his.

"You're too sweet, my beautiful girl," he whispers before kissing my temple. "Honestly, I think the harder part was adjusting to civilian life when I got out. I always knew I wouldn't be in the military forever, but it becomes your whole world and community all wrapped up in one. I was aimless for a while. Restless. Just sort of... drifting," he says thoughtfully.

"And then you came here and took over the bar?"

"Something like that. Grams can be very convincing."

"So I hear," I say with a smile. Hudson returns it, the playful sparkle in his eyes heating me up from the inside out. "You can be pretty convincing too, you know."

"Is that right?" he murmurs, leaning forward to ghost his lips up my neck.

"Mmhm," I answer breathlessly, tilting my head to the side to give him better access.

Hudson growls and licks a sensitive spot below my ear, making me shiver. I turn, capturing his lips with mine. He pauses at first like he can't believe I'd initiate anything. Doubt flashes through me, but then Hudson lets out a painful groan and hauls me onto his lap, spearing his tongue inside my mouth.

"I'm too heavy!" I shriek, but Hudson isn't having any of that.

"You're fucking perfect," he grunts, his hands roaming down my back and squeezing my ass appreciatively.

"Hardly," I breathe out, spreading my legs wider so I can grind down harder.

"Sydney, I mean it," Hudson says more seriously, pulling back from me. "Do you need me to show you?"

"What... what do you mean?"

Hudson tips his head back, a jagged groan filling the apartment.

"Can I touch you? Everywhere? I fucking need to watch you come again, on my fingers this time. Fill up my hand with your sweet release."

I rub my lips together, staring into those intense blue eyes. Hudson cups my face and brushes this thumb across my lips, encouraging me to release them. As soon as I do, he presses a soft kiss on my mouth, then nuzzles into my neck.

"Yes, please," I finally say, my voice barely above a whisper.

It's enough to get Hudson's attention, though. He stands up with me in his arms, making me giggle as I cling to him. Hudson carries me as if I weigh nothing, kissing me the whole time.

We don't make it very far before Hudson presses me against the nearest wall and kisses down my neck. I look up into his deep blue eyes, seeing a desire so bright and hot it should scare me away. Instead, it heats me up from the inside out, making me bold in my desperation for more.

I slide my hands up his neck, tangling my fingers into his slightly shaggy, perfectly messy hair. Pulling him down, I initiate the kiss this time, breathing him in and melting against him. Hudson growls into my mouth, gripping my ass and helping me grind against his hard cock, creating just enough friction to drive me insane. It's not enough. I need more.

Whimpering into his mouth, I cling to him, molding myself against his body, trying to climb this beast of a man. He growls again and hikes me up higher in his arms, using his body to press me against the wall as he rubs his thickness against my core. I let out a moan, tipping my head back as I shamelessly squeeze my thighs around his hips and grind my pulsing, dripping pussy against him.

"Jesus," he grunts into the side of my neck before kissing me there. "I can feel your heat."

All I can do is whimper as he takes my mouth once more in a searing kiss. The next thing I know, I'm being carried and then placed on a hard surface. Breaking the kiss, I look around and realize I'm sitting on the kitchen counter. Hudson steps between my legs and nuzzles into my neck, his hands gripping my hips in a bruising hold. I love it. I want his mark. I don't even care how messed up that sounds.

Hudson breathes against my mouth, his thumb pulling my chin down. He fills my mouth with his breath once, twice, then a slow, rolling lick of his tongue. A shudder wracks his body and he grabs my knees, spreading them wide and jerking me to the edge of the counter.

"Your lips are so fucking sweet," he murmurs before diving back in. His hands trail up my thighs, pushing my dress up higher and higher. I whimper into his mouth, then gasp when his thumbs brush against my lacy panties.

"M-more," I stutter out, unable to hide the desperate tone in my shaky voice.

"So wet for me," Hudson grunts. His lips brush against the shell of my ear, making me shiver. Even just that light, teasing touch makes me ache for so much more. "Can I touch you, beautiful? Can I make you come again?"

I nod my head and wiggle my hips, trying to get him right where I'm hurting the most. "Please," I whisper, fisting his shirt.

Hudson doesn't waste a single second. He presses his thumb against my panty-covered pussy, rubbing my clit in light, teasing circles. The lacy fabric scrapes against my sensitive bundle of nerves, making me jerk forward and press my face against the side of his neck. Hudson grunts in approval then slips his hand under the waistband and touches me for real.

I bury my face deeper into his neck, muffling the loud moan that escapes my lips. His fingers slide through my soaking wet folds, stroking me up and down but never quite touching me where I need him the most. I tilt my hips, seeking relief, but Hudson just chuckles darkly.

"You need something from me?"

"Mmhm," is about all I can say at the moment.

"Need me to fingerfuck this tight, wet little pussy?"

"Y-yesss," I moan.

"Need me to make you come?"

I nod my head, then gasp and fall forward into his chest as he rubs the rough pad of his finger over my clit. Hudson grunts in approval before crashing his lips down on mine. I immediately open up for him, letting him take control. I'm at his mercy, completely surrendered to the pleasure only he can bring.

When his thick finger circles my pulsing entrance, I cry out, the jagged, broken sound echoing around the tiny room. I feel myself tense and release, more of my arousal dripping out of me and coating his hand.

"God, Sydney. So fucking responsive," he whispers, more to himself than to me.

I have no idea what I'm doing, but my body does, some primal instinct taking over as lust trickles through every vein, every cell, hitting me deep in my core. Releasing my hold on him, I lean back, setting my hands down on the counter behind me. I open my legs wider and tip my head back, letting him do whatever he wants to me.

He growls, the savage sound rattling my bones and making me impossibly wetter for him. Hudson leans over me, biting down on my exposed neck as his finger thrusts into me, stretching me wide open.

"Shit, baby. How are you so damn tight?" he groans.

I don't have a voice, let alone an answer for him. Hudson slowly slides in and out of me while grinding the heel of his hand against my clit. I arch my back, shoving my cunt down on his finger, silently begging for more. Hudson gladly obliges. He shoves two fingers inside me, curling them up and stroking some incredibly sensitive spot over and over.

"Oh God," I whimper.

"That's it, beautiful. I feel you. I feel this tight little cunt squeezing me so damn good. I know you want to come for me."

All I can do is whimper. My soft, urgent cries grow louder and louder as the pressure deep in my core expands and pushes all the air out of my lungs. Hudson leans over me and winds his fingers in my hair while still owning my pleasure and my pussy with his other hand.

He tugs gently but firmly on my long locks, forcing my gaze to meet his. Hungry, almost feral blue eyes stare back at me. Our heavy breaths mingle, his lips barely touching mine.

"Come for me, Sydney. Come on my fingers. Fill my hand up with your release. I want it all. It's mine."

His dirty words make me shiver and spread my legs wider, wanting that. Wanting to obey him. Wanting to give him everything he demands of me.

"I-I-I'm..."

"Yes, fuck yes," he groans right before swallowing down my cries of pleasure.

There's a deep tugging in my lower belly, followed by an incredible, painful, blissful rush of liquid heat. All at once, my orgasm erupts from my core, wave after wave of molten lava flooding my body, singeing my nerves as I spasm and jerk and gasp for air.

Hudson groans, his fist tightening in my hair while his other hand never lets up its assault on my pussy. He doesn't slow down, doesn't let me catch my breath before a second orgasm splinters into the first one.

My arms and legs shake and then go numb. All I can feel are his fingers scissoring inside of me, stretching, stroking, owning me completely.

I'm drained of every damn thing when he pulls his hand out of my pussy, nearly collapsing on top of the counter. Hudson grins, a dark, satisfied gleam in his eyes. I'm shocked when he lifts his fingers to his lips and sucks off my juices. A whimper falls from my lips when he closes his eyes and growls.

Hudson pulls me up and kisses me, letting me taste myself on his tongue. I'm still out of breath and trembling when we break apart.

I'm not sure what comes over me, but suddenly, I want to taste him. Need it. My body moves on its own before my brain can catch up. I slide off the counter and get down on my knees. I have no idea what I'm doing, I just know that I want to do it. I *need* to do it. Hudson looks down at me with wide eyes, dark with lust.

"You don't have to—" His words die on his lips, swallowed up by a loud groan when I rub my palm up and down his huge, hard dick.

I look up at him, satisfied beyond reason that his face is twisted up in pleasure. Working quickly, I undo his belt and zipper, eager to touch him the way he touched me.

"Wow," I whisper, feeling foolish as soon as the word leaves my mouth. I'm sure I look and sound stupid, but I can't help it. He's huge. I can barely wrap my fingers around his thickness. The desperate, devilish ache in my core rises when I see a drop of white, pearly liquid form on the tip of his throbbing cock.

I lean forward and lick it up, gasping at the salty, earthy flavor. Hudson growls, which makes me moan and wrap my lips around him. God, he barely fits in my mouth, but I want more. I swirl my tongue around the head, rubbing my tongue along the little slit on top. He grunts, sounding almost like he's in pain.

I keep exploring him, licking the large vein on the underside of his cock, teasing him with kisses, then finally swallowing him down again, choking on his length. Hudson tangles his fingers in my hair, holding me still. I can't tell if he wants me to stop or go deeper. I know what I want, and I don't want to stop.

"Sydney," he growls, tightening his hold on my hair. The strands pull against my scalp, the slight sting hitting me right between my legs. "Fuck, you're incredible."

I beam up at him, unreasonably proud of his praise. It makes me want more. More of his words, more of his cock, just... more. Relaxing my jaw, I slide down another inch, then another, until he hits the back of my throat.

Hudson cups the side of my face, holding me still. I look up at him and see a need so great, so desperate, I know I'm going to do whatever he asks of me to satisfy him. Slowly, Hudson moves his hips, pulling out of me then pressing back in. I suck him down, hollowing out my cheeks as he takes control, fucking my mouth.

"Jesus," he grunts, snapping his hips. He's thrusting in and out of me faster now, rougher than before. I take all of it, everything he's giving me. I feel a surge of pride when he starts shaking, clearly losing control.

My hands move on their own, reaching up to grab his ass and keep him deep inside my mouth. Hudson lets out a string of curse words as his dick twitches and swells up. I suck him down further, the tip of his cock popping into the back of my throat. Hudson trembles almost violently, then bursts inside me, his hot cum trickling down my throat in forceful waves. I moan and drink down every last drop before licking him clean.

Sitting back on my heels, I wipe my mouth with the back of my hand and look up at this beast of a man. He's breathing heavily and staring at me like I'm a goddess. I feel like one in this moment. His goddess. I feel powerful and sexy for the first time in my life. It's addicting.

"Goddamn," Hudson pants, running a hand through his hair. He helps me up off the floor and carries me over to the couch, settling in with me on his lap. I curl up on his chest, perfectly content.

Hudson strokes my back as I bury my face against the side of his neck, breathing in his peppermint scent now mixed with sweat and the remnants of his release.

"That was incredible, sweet girl," he whispers, kissing the top of my head. "I wasn't expecting that at all. I hope you didn't feel pressured to... God, I couldn't live with myself if—"

"I liked it," I blurt out awkwardly, sitting up from where I was nestled on his chest. "I, um, I didn't feel pressure. I just wanted to make you feel good. Did it feel good?"

"Did it... fucking hell, it was the best thing that's ever happened to my dick."

I laugh at the serious expression on his face, then yawn. Hudson chuckles and guides me so we're snuggling closer than ever. I'm so spent after all the orgasms, that I allow my eyelids to flutter shut. Just for now. It's too hard to resist when I feel safer and more loved than ever, right here in Hudson's arms.

Chapter Nine

Hudson

I'm wiping down the bar, grinning like a fool in love. That's not far off from the truth. I already know Sydney is the one for me, and I think she's finally starting to get it, too.

"What's got you smiling so big?"

I look up to see an old friend from high school, Dylan, saunter up to the bar. "Look what the cat dragged in," I half joke. The man looks rough. He's always been strikingly handsome, at least according to the girls we grew up with. It's been a few years since we've seen each other, but he looks tired and frazzled.

"Yeah, well, not all of us live a charming, uncomplicated life in a cutesy small town," he grumbles.

"Good to see you too, buddy," I say, pouring him a shot of whiskey. "On the house. You look like you could use a drink and a shoulder to cry on."

Dylan glares at me before swallowing down the shot and smacking the glass on the bar top. "Save your shoulder and get me another shot."

"That bad, huh?"

"Pretty bad, yeah."

"Did you just come here for the free booze? Seems like a long way to travel. I'm sure they have bars in Denver."

"I needed to get out of the city for a bit. I didn't mean to end up here, it just sort of happened. I remember you saying you moved here after getting out of the military. Stopped by the gas station up the road and asked about you. The guy sent me over here, and well..." He shrugs and starts fiddling with the empty shot glass.

"It's good to see you, no matter the circumstances. Anything you want to talk about?"

"No." He sighs and runs a hand through his thick black hair. "Yes. It's... fuck, I can't even say it."

"Is everything okay? Do you need help? Money or something?"

"No, no. I'm a tenured professor with a dozen medical equipment patents under my name, remember? I wish it were money problems, though. Those can be fixed easily enough. But this... shit, I think I've got it bad for a student."

I nod my head, trying not to show my surprise. Dylan and I haven't hung out in person in years, but we've traded emails and phone calls. I know he takes his job seriously and wouldn't do anything stupid to jeopardize it.

"Does she feel the same way?" I ask.

Dylan gives me a sharp look. "It doesn't matter how she feels. Sarah is young and in a vulnerable position. She just looks up to me, that's all. I got her out of a bad situation, and now she sees me as some sort of hero."

I nod my head again, letting him talk it out with himself. This is how Dylan operates when he's this worked up. He doesn't really want a conversation; he wants a sounding board.

"And then there's the power dynamic," he continues. "Not only is she my student, she's my... fuck, I don't know. It's more than lust. I want to protect her and watch over her. I want to be the one she comes to when she has problems and when she's scared. I've never been this possessive over anyone and it's driving me insane. Fuck," he growls.

"Have you told her any of this?"

"It's... complicated."

"So you've said."

"I want her," he says softly, looking down at the glass in his hand as he twirls it around. "Need her. Feels like I can't breathe without her."

I get it. I feel the same way about my Sydney. The few days she was refusing me and running away from me were pure torture. I can't imagine having to fight my feelings for someone totally off-limits.

"Well, it sounds like you need to make a decision, then. It's not fair to either of you to keep her in limbo. You need to either claim her or let her go."

"Let her go? Let her run into the arms of another man? Let her live her life without me there to watch over her?" The anger ripples off of him, like the very thought of not having her in his life is repulsive and offensive.

"I think you have your answer," I say with a smirk.

Dylan is about to come back with a smart-ass retort, just like the good old days, but then his phone rings. "Dammit, I need to take this. Coffee for the road?"

"Sure thing. And don't be a stranger. Stop by for a real visit next time."

"I will. I'm sorry I just stumbled in here to rant. We'll hang out soon."

I nod and hand him his coffee as he races out the door. Damn, I can't wait to see what happens there. Right now, however, I need to check on my woman.

I lean against the door to the back office, watching Sydney write something down on a pad of paper before entering it into the computer. She's so damn beautiful. I can't believe she's here, helping me redecorate the bar. Surely I'm just wishing it into being.

I almost convinced myself our date didn't happen the other night since it was too good to be true. God, the way she took her pleasure, rocked her hips, and creamed all over my hand drove me wild with lust. And then the goddess got on her knees and gave me the greatest gift in the world.

I swallow down a growl, trying not to get a full-on erection at work. Sydney must have heard me, because she lifts her head, her green eyes meeting mine.

"Hey," she says with a smile that melts my heart. I stalk toward her, unable to keep my distance any longer. "I was just about to go find you.

I have some options for new light fixtures, but I want to make sure it's still within the budget—oh!"

She makes the cutest little squeaking noise as I pull the desk chair back and lean over her, resting my hands on the armrests.

"Hi, beautiful," I murmur before claiming her lips. Fuck, I haven't tasted her since she got here this morning. Nearly seven hours ago. Far too long to go without a hit of my new favorite drug.

"Hi," she answers once I release her from our kiss.

I start to pull away, but Sydney fists my shirt and pulls me back, her teeth sinking into my bottom lip before she tugs it and then slips her tongue inside my mouth.

"Fuck," I grunt against her swollen lips, diving back in for more. "Need something from me, sweetheart?"

Sydney nods. "You can't just come in here all... all... well, like this, and expect me to just let you go," she says exasperatedly. Her adorable pout mixed with undeniable lust has my dick jerking in my jeans, already dribbling precum at the thought of giving my sweet girl every single inch.

"I never want you to let me go," I say softly as I leave little love bites up and down her neck. "What do you need?" I grunt harshly into the shell of her ear as she squirms beneath me. "My fingers?" Sydney whimpers and arches her back in the chair, her ample breasts scraping against my chest. "How about my tongue?"

"Yes," she moans loudly. "And... and..."

"And?" I growl, wedging myself between her legs and resting my forehead against hers.

Sydney looks a little lost and overwhelmed, but she's so fucking turned on and desperate for me it looks painful. Christ, I can relive that ache. But I want her to be sure.

"There's no pressure," I whisper, trying with all my might to sound comforting instead of like the raging beast I feel like right now. "I can make you come so many different ways without using my cock." Sydney moans and wiggles her hips, grinding her wet core against my leg.

"M-maybe you could..." Sydney pauses, and for a moment, I think she's not going to tell me what she wants. I see the moment she realizes the power she has over me. She knows I'd bow down and worship her if she only gave me a chance. "I think I want to c-come on your t-tongue," she whispers.

"Fuck," I groan. I love that she trusted me with this. Her voice may be tentative, but there's no mistaking her intentions when she pushes me back and stands up, flinging herself in my arms.

I haul her curvy, sexy fucking body up against mine, taking the opportunity to squeeze her soft flesh and revel in how perfect she is.

Setting her down on the desk, I urge Sydney to lay down. She gives me a questioning look but does what I want. My hands skim up her bare thighs, underneath the hem of her dress. I stroke her juicy cunt, groaning when I feel the soaking wet fabric of her panties.

Without wasting another second, I kneel down in front of her and peel the scrap of fabric down her legs, tossing it aside. Sydney gasps and then moans for me as I lick her up and down. I suck on her folds, dipping my tongue into every crease, memorizing everything about her. Her legs twitch and snap around my head, but I place my hands on the insides of her thighs and spread her wide open for me again.

I dip my tongue into her tight hole, pulling out more of her sweet juices. My baby is fucking gushing for me. I want to taste every inch of her. I force my tongue out of her entrance and pull her juices up, up, up to her clit, flicking my tongue over her tight bundle of nerves just once.

"Ohmygod!" she yells as her hips buck against my mouth.

I grunt and suck on her clit while she trembles at the tip of my tongue. Slowly, I slip a finger into her tight little hole, pumping in and out in a steady rhythm. Her hands grip the edge of the desk as she hangs on for dear life.

I curl my finger up, finding her G-spot while working my tongue over her clit, licking and sucking and bringing her higher and higher. I can feel her tensing, her body strung so fucking tight. I want to feel her snap.

"Come for me, beautiful. Fucking come all over my face," I growl.

When I add a second finger, Sydney screams my name and bows her back off the desk, writhing and crying out her orgasm. Her pussy pulses, gripping my fingers and sucking them further inside. I stroke her pussy lightly, bringing her back down to earth.

Licking my fingers clean, I stand, looking down at my woman. She's gasping for air, flushed, sweating, and just so goddamn gorgeous.

"Holy crap," she breathes out, making me grin. "That was amazing. Like... wow. Wow," she says again, struggling to sit up.

I chuckle and gather her into my arms, not even bothering to grab her panties from the floor as I carry her upstairs to my apartment. I'll come back for them later. Right now, we both need something else.

Once inside my apartment, I stride toward my bedroom and set her down, cupping my sweet girl's face. She's still a little worn out from the orgasm I just gave her, and hell if that isn't the biggest turn-on ever. I can't wait to give her more.

"Tell me what you want," I whisper, nuzzling into the top of her head.

"Whatever you want," comes her soft reply. Sydney rubs herself against me, making me growl.

"You know I want everything," I grit out, dropping my hands from her face so I can mold them to her ass and help her grind down. "I want all of you. Want to feel that pussy squeeze the life out of my cock as I tunnel in and out of you. Want to hear how you sound when your man claims you from the inside out. Want your cries of pleasure ringing in my ears as I send you up and over again and again and again..."

"Yes," she moans, her hands tugging at my shirt as if she can't wait another second.

"Are you sure, Sydney? I'm going out of my damn mind, and I need to know you're all in before I snap completely."

She surprises me by lifting her hands to my face and pressing the sweetest kiss on my nose. Her green eyes peer right down into my soul, and she only hesitates for a second before telling me what's on her mind. "I've never, uh, done it before. Sex. Or... anything. You're my only experience so far and I don't want you to be disapp—"

I cut her off with a hungry kiss, unwilling to hear the rest of that ridiculous word. Disappointed? Never.

"I'll be so good to you, sweet girl," I rasp against her lips. "Love that I'm the first. The only. Promise me," I demand. She nods frantically, then tightens her grip on my shirt. "Good," I grunt. She pauses, chewing on her bottom lip. Without her asking, I already know what her question is. "Can't remember anyone before you, Sydney. It's been... fuck, ten years? Longer, maybe. You'll be my everything, my beautiful Sydney. You already are."

Sydney's eyes twinkle, and she nods, letting me know my answer was a good one. Thank fucking Christ. Maybe I'm getting better with my words.

When her green irises flash with a dark, lust-filled spark, my already painfully hard cock surges and twitches in my pants. "Show me what it means to be yours."

I growl and spin her around so her back is facing me. I find the zipper on the back of her dress and slowly pull it down, kissing every inch of skin revealed to me. When she's completely unzipped, I drag my lips and nose up her spine and kiss the back of her neck, making her shiver.

Carefully, reverently, I slip the straps off her shoulders and watch as the dress pools at her feet. I lean down and kiss her neck again while reaching for the clip in her hair. My beautiful girl is standing before me completely naked, her dark silky hair handing over her shoulders.

"Turn around for me," I purr. She hesitates for a second, but then slowly she spins around, showing off her breathtaking body. I don't even think she realizes how seductive she's being, which makes me want her all the more.

I can see her fighting off the urge to cover herself up, but I'm so damn proud that she doesn't. She lets me see all of her. I can't get enough of her large, perky breasts, her wide hips, the soft curve of her belly.

I let my fingertips wander over the creamy skin of her shoulders and down the sides of her juicy, bouncy tits. Then I take one in each hand, squeezing them gently. Sydney moans softly for me and then gasps as I tease her already hard nipples.

"Fucking perfect. You were made for me," I whisper before capturing her lips in a wild kiss. I walk her back toward the bed, kissing her the whole way. When her calves hit the edge of the mattress, I give her a slight push, making her laugh quietly as her back hits the soft sheets.

Sydney crawls up the bed and sits up on her elbows, watching me with an excited heat in her eyes. "I wanna see you too," she pouts.

I growl and begin ripping at my clothes, needing her skin on my skin as quickly as possible. "Touch yourself, beautiful. Make that sweet pussy come."

Her cheeks turn pink and then red, but her hand slides down in between her legs. I love that she trusts me even though she's a little nervous and out of her element. I want to push her boundaries but make sure she feels safe the whole time.

I watch, mesmerized as Sydney circles her fingers around her clit and stares right at me. Fuck, she's so goddamn sexy, my little vixen spread out for me. I peel my shirt off and I can fucking *see* her pussy throb as a wave of her juices trickles out of her.

"Oh my God, Hudson..." she breaths out. "You're..." She bites her lip and turns bright red again, the blush spreading to her chest.

"What am I?" I ask as I undo my pants and let them drop to the floor.

"You're perfect. I can't believe you want me."

It pains me that she doesn't see her own beauty. I plan to fix that, starting right the fuck now. Gripping my cock, I squeeze the fucker in long, hard strokes to relieve some of this pressure building up inside. "See how much I want you? You did this to me."

"Show me," she whispers, echoing her earlier words while rubbing her clit. "Show me how much you want me."

"Anything for you," I grit out before climbing on top of her. I replace her hand with mine, rubbing her and groaning when I feel her warm honey drip all over my hand.

Sydney reaches down and strokes my dick, spreading the steady stream of precum up and down my shaft. "I need you, Hudson. Please, please..."

I remove her hand and rock my thick, hard cock up and down her slit, gathering up her juices and bumping her clit again and again. I position myself right at her entrance and hover there, feeling her pulsing little hole massage the head of my dick.

"Ready for me, my beautiful Sydney?"

She looks me right in the eye with equal parts trust and trepidation. I kiss her softly, hoping to ease some of her worry.

"I'm ready, Hudson. I want to feel all of you. Please make love to me."

Her words course through my veins and settle deep into my heart. This goddess is offering herself up to me, giving me her virginity even though I've messed up so many times with her already. I'll never take her trust for granted.

I ease my way into her tight little channel and swallow her whimpers in an all-consuming kiss. "Relax, angel. Let me take care of you," I whisper onto her lips. I circle her clit with my thumb as I gently stretch her open in shallow thrusts.

When she's nice and relaxed for me, I pull back all the way and fill her up to the hilt, breaking through her innocence and making her mine forever.

"Mine, all fucking mine," I growl right before kissing away the lone tear falling down her cheek.

"Yours," she whimpers.

I hate that she's in pain, but I can't help the caveman that comes out in me. I want to beat my chest and roar out to the universe that I've found my mate for life. Instead, I stay completely still, buried deep inside her perfect cunt, letting her get used to me.

Sydney wiggles beneath me, the movement lodging my cock deeper inside of her, making us both groan.

"Shit, beautiful, you feel so fucking good. Take it slow, baby. We have forever."

"I need more, Hudson. Please?" She leans up to kiss me, her arms looping around my neck and pulling me down on top of her.

I want to be gentle, but I'm only so strong. Her perfect, warm, soaking cunt is wrapped around me so tight, sucking me back in even as I pull out of her and thrust back inside.

"Oh God, oh God yes, more," she moans, bucking her hips slightly and testing out how we fit together.

It's too damn good. I snap my hips a little more forcefully than I intended and worry for a second that I hurt her sensitive, swollen, freshly broken in pussy.

"Don't stop," she cries out, putting all of my worries at ease and making me growl at her eager, desperate tone.

There's a quiet, reverent rhythm to the way I move inside her body and the way she receives me. She strokes my back and kisses my neck.

And then something switches. Her fingernails drag down my back and she bites my shoulder, marking me and making me snarl into her mouth as I take her lips in a punishing kiss. I respond with a rough thrust that makes her breasts bounce.

"Don't stop," she cries out, louder, more forceful this time.

I don't. I lose myself in her, fucking her hard and dirty, our skin slapping together, her wet pussy making deliciously sloppy sounds as I pull out and slam back into her again and again.

"Fuck, Sydney, this pussy is heaven. So tight and perfect for me," I grunt out.

Sydney gasps as her pussy starts to choke my dick. She's about to come, I can feel it. I pick up my speed and lean down to suck on her gorgeous tits. She lets out a jagged moan and tangles her fingers in my hair, holding me to her breasts as I feast on them.

"Hudson, oh God, I'm... I think... I'm gonna..."

"Come for me right the fuck now," I growl, looking at her beautiful face as she races towards her climax.

Sydney sucks in a sharp breath and holds it, her body going still, her muscles straining and tensing as I pound into that sweet pussy again and again.

All at once, she lets go of all the tension coiling in her body. Sydney spasms around me, her cunt squeezing the life out of my cock while she writhes beneath me and arches her back. I fuck her through it, sucking on her nipples and grabbing her juicy ass, holding her in place so I can drill her into the mattress.

My girl keeps coming and coming, releasing her sweet honey all over my dick. Her pussy is still throbbing when I pull out of her. She whimpers at the loss, but I flip her over on her stomach and position her on all fours.

"Jesus, fuck, so beautiful like this," I praise her. My dirty girl wiggles her voluptuous ass and I smack it, growling as her cheeks jiggle. Sydney moans and bucks her hips back.

I spank her one more time and then grip her cheeks in my hands, prying her open so I can see her dripping wet opening. Without warning, I plunge back into her, hitting home in one rough thrust.

"Oh fuck, Hudson you're so, so deep," she cries out.

I grip her hips and bounce her luscious body off my cock while she moans and grips the sheets. My sweet, filthy girl screams and comes again, her orgasm rippling through her body and pulsing around my dick. I can't hold on much longer, but I want to feel this, feel her wrapped around me as long as I can.

"One more, Sydney, give me one more," I demand, my voice low and urgent as I snap my hips.

I loop one arm under her hips, holding her up as I fuck her savagely. Reaching out with my other hand, I fist her hair, riding her with every goddamn thing I have. Sydney sobs her release, gushing all over me, jerking in my arms as I hold her up. I grind my cock so deep inside of her, feeling her pussy massage me.

Finally, I give myself permission to let go. With a roar, I empty rope after rope of sticky, hot cum inside of her. My dick hurts so good with the force of each new wave. I fill her up to the brim and then keep going, my orgasm stretching out longer, harder than I've ever experienced. My seed dribbles out of her, coating her thighs, my balls, and the bed below.

With one last thrust and a primal grunt, I empty the last of my cum deep inside of her. She collapses on the bed, effectively dislodging my shaft from her warmth.

I look down and see the evidence of her virginity smeared over my softening cock. Only then do I come back into my body and realize I just tore her apart viciously, almost violently during her first time. Panic lances my heart and I find it hard to breathe.

I lay down next to her and cup her face so gently, the way I should have treated her all along.

"Sydney, God, are you okay?"

She opens her eyes and smiles at me, half dazed. "So, so good," she mumbles, turning her head to kiss my palm.

"Thank fuck," I breathe out before wrapping her up in my arms and holding her close. "Jesus, you're amazing. I've never experienced anything like that, Sydney. Only you, only you baby. Only you can do that to me."

She sighs dreamily, easing more of my worry until all I can feel is whole and happy.

We stay like that for long moments, both of us coming down from our high and recalibrating after that all-consuming experience. I finally break the silence, wanting to know everything about my girl.

"Did you always want to be an interior designer?" I ask.

"Not at first. I didn't even know what an interior designer did until I was in high school," she says, chuckling at herself. "But I took a design class offered at the community college my senior year and realized what a difference things like color and lighting make in a room. I like looking at a space and figuring out how I can make it more efficient or how I can improve the overall mood of a room. It's like a puzzle, kind of."

I nod my head, fascinated with how her mind works. "Do you want to own your own business?"

"No," she answers right away, shaking her head against my chest.

"Why not?"

"It's too... I don't know. Too much. I'm not a leader, I'm more of a behind-the-scenes person."

"You're doing an excellent job tackling The Pink Door all on your own. I think you'd make a great business owner."

Sydney shakes her head no again. "It's too risky. I'm too young and inexperienced. Plus, I don't like being the center of attention. I'd much rather do the heavy lifting in the background."

"Even if it means your work will get looked over? Or someone else takes credit for your ideas?" I'm not judging Sydney, I just want to know what she's thinking. I know my girl is shy, but I would hate for her to keep her talent and passion hidden.

"There are pros and cons to everything," she says with a shrug.

"You have people around here who would love your help. You already have a job with me, and I know you've been helping out the

Hendersons, as well as others around town. That has to be some good experience, right?"

"Yeah, but..." she sighs, and I know I need to stop pushing.

"It's okay, beautiful. I didn't mean to upset you. I just wish you could see how incredible you are."

Sydney snuggles deeper into my chest while I run my fingers through her hair and kiss her forehead. She tries pulling away from me, and I realize she doesn't want me to see the scar there.

"Hey," I whisper softly, tucking her hair behind her ear so I can see her face. "You never have to hide any part of yourself from me, sweetheart. I want it all." Sydney furrows her brow, then nods. Her muscles relax and she sinks further into my embrace. "When you're ready, I would be honored to hear how you got this," I murmur, pressing another kiss over her scar.

Sydney inhales deeply and then lets it all out in one big sigh. She deflates against me and I tighten my hold on her, letting her know I'm not going anywhere.

"I was in a house fire when I was four," she starts. I hold my breath, soaking up the pain from each softly spoken word. "I don't remember it much, just the chaos, the heat, the blinding light. I was trapped in my room and didn't know how to get out or even call for help."

"Sydney," I murmur, pressing kisses on her head, her cheeks, anywhere I can reach.

"A firefighter found me, though I don't know how long I was in that cramped room with flames and smoke suffocating me. When he broke down the door with his ax, a few pieces of wood and shrapnel flew out and cut my face and arms. This one was the worst," she finishes, pointing to her scar. I kiss it.

"I'm so sorry, sweetheart. So sorry you went through that. Did anyone else get hurt?"

She nods, and my stomach sinks. "Both of my parents. They didn't make it out. I moved in with my grandma the next day."

Sydney sniffles and I surround her with my strength, rocking her back and forth. She's been through so much, and yet here she is, secure in my arms. I'll protect this precious woman and make sure no one and nothing harms a hair on her head ever again.

"Thank you for trusting me," I whisper as I stroke her back.

"Thank you for being trustworthy," she murmurs before snuggling closer.

My heart squeezes up in my chest, then pumps a surge of love and tenderness throughout my body as I look down at Sydney. She's it for me. I just hope I can get her to agree.

"Sleep now," I say softly as I pull the blankets over us.

"Mmhm, just for a little bit," Sydney replies. She yawns, stretches, and then curls up against me like the most adorable cat. Yeah, this woman is so fucking mine.

Chapter Ten

Sydney

I wake up surrounded by Hudson's peppermint and pine scent. His arms are wrapped around me, holding me close. Light peeks in through the curtain, and I can tell it's still early. As much as I'd like to stay here forever, I really need a drink of water. My throat is scratchy, probably from shouting Hudson's name all night.

Holy freaking crap, it was incredible. My body heats up at the memory of his massive length sliding in and out of me, stretching me and hitting me just right. I squeeze my thighs together, hoping to relieve some of the pressure between them.

Hopefully, I'll be getting more of that soon. But first, water.

I wiggle my way out of Hudson's hold, smiling to myself when he grunts and reaches out for me again. I slip a pillow into his arms, barely suppressing a laugh as he snuggles into it. This muscled god of a man is unbearably adorable, even vulnerable in the early morning light.

Tiptoeing out of the room, I grab Hudson's shirt off the floor and pull it over my head. I make a mad dash to the kitchen, wanting to be back in bed with Hudson as soon as possible. I grab a glass and fill it up with water, gulping it down before refilling it.

"Thirsty?"

Hudson's deep, scratchy morning voice makes my knees weak. Everything about him causes white-hot lust to burn through my veins, especially when he's stalking toward me with such a dark, devilish look in his eyes.

I set my cup down on the counter right as Hudson, completely naked, pulls me against his hard body and slants his lips over mine. Hudson feasts on me, each swipe of his tongue pulling more and more pleasure out of me until I'm shaking with the need for release.

I moan into his mouth, breaking our kiss. Hudson fists my hair and pulls my head up, exposing my neck. His teeth, tongue, and lips devour every inch of skin from my jaw down to my shoulder.

"Please, Hudson, I need more..."

He growls into my skin as his hands roam all over my body. One grips my ass and squeezes, while the other slides down my front, lifting up the hem of the shirt I'm wearing. His fingers trail up my thigh, up, up, up, until they graze over my slit.

"You're so fucking wet."

"Mmm..." Is all I can manage to say.

Hudson slides two fingers up and down my slit. We both moan at the same time, and he rubs my clit in the most incredible way, making my knees shake and my entire body tense. I grab his biceps and dig my fingers in, needing him to keep me steady while he assaults my throbbing pussy.

His fingers thrust inside of me at the same time he slams his lips into mine. The kiss is fire and fury; sweetness and release. He's stretching me out, pain and pleasure mixing, as the heel of his hand grinds down on my clit. I shamelessly buck my hips into his hand, needing more, needing everything.

My body is strung so tight, my legs shake, my fingers clench, and my pussy leaks all over his hand. I break our kiss and drop my head to his shoulder, unable to even breathe as he brings me to heights unknown with just his fingers alone.

"That's it, Sydney. I love when you come for me."

He pulls his fingers out of my channel and rubs them over my clit in tight, demanding circles. His fingers slide over my bundle of nerves one more time and that's all it takes for the pleasure to break over me like a waterfall. Rivulets of pleasure run through my body, on the inside of my skin, as every muscle jerks again and again.

Hudson holds me close to him, crushing me against his body to keep me grounded as the orgasm rocks through me. I cling to him as I tense and release one final time.

"Jesus, you're amazing," he whispers.

Even though I just had a mind-blowing orgasm, my pussy clenches around his hand that's still buried deep inside of me. Hudson groans and pumps his fingers inside of me one more time before taking his hand away and licking himself clean.

"Goddamn, I need a better taste of you right the fuck now, sweetheart."

Before I can respond, Hudson tugs the shirt over my head and then scoops me up in his arms, running toward the bedroom while I laugh breathlessly. He lays me down on the bed so gently, like I'm the precious thing to him. One look in those deep blue eyes, and I know it's true.

His gaze travels up and down my body, spread out for him on the mattress. A savage look takes over his features, making my pussy ache and squeeze around nothing. I need him inside me again, need to feel him move deep within me, need to surrender to his control.

My stunning, sweet, sexy Hudson kneels in front of me, then grabs my ankles and throws one leg over his shoulder, followed by the other. Some sort of pained grumble comes from Hudson as he stares right into the core of me.

"*Fuuuuuck.*"

It's the last thing I hear before his tongue dips into my folds and he licks me up and down. My hips twitch and my thighs snap shut around his head. Hudson groans, sending delicious waves of vibrations over my body and setting every nerve ending on high alert. Hudson sucks and bites and licks and teases me right to the brink... and then he backs off.

His hands slide under my ass as he pulls me forward, practically suffocating on my core. His tongue spears into my entrance as he licks my walls, lapping at me and sucking down my honey as it drips out of me. It's like the more he tastes, the hungrier he gets.

His thumb rubs over my clit as he keeps thrusting his tongue in and out of me. I'm close, so close, and I know he knows. This time, he lets me fall right over the edge. I pulse and squirm and grab his hair, grinding my pussy deeper into his face as he drinks up my release.

When I finally grow limp, Hudson backs off, giving my pussy one last kiss.

"Delicious," he grunts. "Need more, Sydney."

I nod helplessly, still boneless from my two earth-shattering orgasms.

Hudson chuckles and then climbs on top of me, pinning me on my back. He's kissing down my neck, over my collarbone, down, down, down, until his tongue lashes out at my nipples. I moan as he sucks and nips at the tender flesh, giving each breast the same attention. I feel each rough lick all the way down in my clit.

My fingers tangle in his hair and I tug his head up so he's looking at me. "Please," I whisper. "I need you inside me."

Hudson growls and nudges my legs apart. I eagerly open up for him. He places a forearm down on either side of my head and kisses me sweetly. And then not so sweetly.

The head of his cock nudges in my entrance, just barely breaching my opening. And then he thrusts inside, claiming me once again.

He slowly pulls out of me as my pussy pulses around his thickness. When he enters me, Hudson growls with such depth it shakes me to the marrow of my bones. I hook my legs around his hips and claw at his back, wanting to fuse our bodies together.

"Yes, Hudson, God, yes," I moan.

He grunts and snaps his hips, plunging deep inside of me in one long thrust. Hudson picks up his pace, thrusting harder, stretching me, hitting every single pleasure spot inside of my pussy. I dig my nails into the hard muscles of his back as I pull myself against him in time with his thrusts. Hudson growls and then smashes his lips down on mine, all teeth and tongue and passion.

We work together, building up to something huge. Each time he hits the end of me, it's like I'm being electrocuted with pleasure, my pussy clenching tightly around his hard dick.

"Jesus, fuck, baby, I feel you gushing for me."

"Faster, please, please, please..." My voice breaks into a moan as he pistons in and out of me, inching closer and closer to sweet release.

It feels like my entire body is teetering on the edge. I tense up, squeezing my body around Hudson, my legs crushing his hips, my fingers no doubt leaving marks on his skin as I hold on for dear life.

"Yes, Hudson, God, Hudson..." I babble on and on as I reach the point of no return.

My orgasm starts in my core and radiates out to every limb, every nerve, every cell in my body. I'm shaking, moaning, going out of my mind with pleasure.

"That's it, Sydney. I'm..."

Hudson throws his head back and roars. His cock throbs deep inside of me, his muscles tight and straining with the effort of holding himself up.

We both come down slowly, together, back to earth, back to our bodies. Hudson rolls off of me, pulling me with him and holding me close. We're sweaty and panting and plastered together in the afterglow of that life-changing experience.

"Goddamn, beautiful. Just... Goddamn."

"Yeah," I laugh softly.

"You okay?"

"Mmm. So good," I tell him truthfully.

He nudges my head up and kisses me sweetly. I sigh and nuzzle my head into his chest, feeling so warm and protected.

***

Later that afternoon, I'm sitting in Hudson's office, scrolling through options for reupholstering the stools and booths. We both slept in after our morning tryst, and then Hudson cooked me breakfast. A girl could get used to this treatment.

I smile as I think about how he's kind of perfect. Who would have thought the grumpy bartender who called me a liar and chased me down the street would be my happily ever after?

My phone dings, alerting me to a new email. I open it, dropping my jaw when I read the contents.

Thank you for submitting an application to Thatcher & Dunn Interior Design.

While you don't qualify for a design position, we'd like to offer a job as a receptionist until you gain enough experience to move your way up. Many of our employees start out this way. We're always promoting from within, and hardworking employees tend to move up the ladder fast...

The words grow blurry as tears form and fall down my cheeks. I'm not sure what to feel. I didn't get the design job. No, I wasn't *qualified* for the design job, even though it was an entry-level position.

Disappointment and embarrassment swirl in my gut, and I have to swallow back bile as it burns my throat. They did offer me a job, though, which is more than I have now. My heart sinks at the thought of answering phones and directing clients to other designers instead of working with them myself.

Then again, maybe this is the way the corporate world works. The email said lots of employees start low on the totem pole and work their way up. How long could that take? Six months? A year? I could put up with being a receptionist for a year if it meant I eventually got to be a designer myself. Plus, Thatcher & Dunn Interior Design is a highly sought-after firm, located in the heart of Denver.

New tears sting my eyes, but I blink them away. Denver. If I moved to Denver, I'd have to leave Hudson. He has his business here, and he's just getting things together. I wouldn't ask him to move with me. That would be ridiculous.

I shove my phone in my pocket and stand up, needing some fresh air. The walls start pressing in on me as the humming fluorescent lights burn into my skin and eyes. The humming becomes louder, the lights brighter, the heat and chaos bearing down on me until I can't breathe.

"Sydney!" The voice sounds like it's coming from underwater. "Sydney, baby, what's wrong?"

"Hudson?" I choke out.

I'm surrounded by his familiar scent, and then he engulfs me in his arms, blocking out the light. I rest my head against his chest, letting the steady sound of his heart drown out the ringing in my ears.

I'm aware of Hudson guiding me over to the couch, urging me to sit down. He kneels in front of me, rubbing his hands up and down my thighs in a calming motion. "You're okay, sweetheart," he whispers. "Just breathe for me. You're safe here."

I nod my head and take a deep breath, willing myself to stop shaking. I'm a wreck because of one email. How can I possibly explain everything to Hudson? It's too early in our relationship for him to see me like this.

"That's it, Sydney," he encourages. "I'm right here." I take a few more calming breaths and finally lift my eyes to meet his. Blue eyes filled with concern and fierce protectiveness stare back at me, nearly making me break down in tears again.

"I got a job offer," I say pathetically. Hudson looks confused, and I don't blame him.

"Are you... isn't that... good?"

"Yes. No. Maybe. I don't know." I sniffle miserably and wipe my eyes, trying to find the words to say. "It's at an amazing design firm in Denver."

Hudson's brow furrows, but he quickly schools his face over. "Well, that's not too far away. I have friends who live there. And if it's a good job, I'm really excited for you," he says carefully.

Would he be able to let me go so easily? I'm over here panicking at the thought of not having Hudson in my life, but if he doesn't feel the same, then what's holding me back?

"It's not exactly what I had hoped for," I tell him. "It's basically a secretary position, but there's a lot of potential for growth, and one day I could be a real designer."

"You *are* a real designer," he growls. I flinch at his harsh tone, and Hudson softens immediately. "Sorry, sweetheart. I just hate hearing you talk down about yourself. You are literally designing this bar right now, and I know you have other projects you're working on, too. You already are a designer. Have you thought any more about going out on your own and building up a client base?"

"I'm too young!" I nearly shout. I didn't mean to be so harsh, but my emotions are all over the place. I'm tired of trying to explain this for the fifth time. "And too inexperienced! I can't just start my own business. I'm not that brave. What if I *want* to stay behind the scenes until I'm ready to take on projects of my own?"

Hudson looks shocked at my outburst, but he takes a deep breath and nods like he's absorbing everything I just said.

"Do you? Want to stay behind the scenes?"

"I don't know! Yes. I mean, not forever. I just... I can't right now. I can't... it's too much."

"What's too much?" He leans in, trying to hold my hands, but I'm too overwhelmed.

"This. No, I mean, not us. Maybe. No, I..." my breaths grow choppy as I look up into those deep blue eyes. Hudson looks hurt and bewildered, and I don't blame him. I don't know what I'm saying. That email threw me off and I know I'm overreacting, but I can't slow down.

"Sydney..."

"Stop! Please. I don't know what I want. The receptionist job is safe. I should take it. I won't be getting any better offers."

"You have offers here. That's what I'm trying to tell you. People have noticed your work, and—"

"No, Hudson. I can't start my own business." I shudder at the thought, releasing another wave of tears.

"Why?"

"Because!" I spit out with frustration. "I'm too—"

"The only person who thinks you're too young and inexperienced is you, Sydney. Don't let those excuses hold you back from fulfilling your dreams."

"But I'm not brave enough," I repeat, grasping at any excuse. I don't know why I'm fighting him so hard. My nerves are frayed and the humming is growing louder with each passing second. Hudson looks disappointed in me, and that's my breaking point.

I jump off the couch, nearly knocking Hudson over in the process.

"Sydney, wait!"

I grab my purse and fly out the door, running through the mostly empty bar and shoving my way outside. My feet hit the pavement, carrying me away from The Pink Door and all its troubles.

Only a few seconds pass before the door is flung open, hitting the outside wall as it bounces back. I pick up speed, knowing it's Hudson. He's chasing after me. Again.

Chapter Eleven

Hudson

No way in hell is Sydney getting away from me. I've chased this woman before, but this time, I have no intention of letting her slip through my fingers.

I have no idea what's going on in her head, just that she was overwhelmed and anxious, and I didn't handle it very well. I'll need to do more research on anxiety and talk to my woman about things that help once she's calmed down a bit. For now, I need to do damage control.

"Sydney!" I call after her. She looks at me over her shoulder, her green eyes holding such sorrow in nearly cracks my heart in two.

When she whips her head back around, she loses her balance, slipping on the pavement. I'm by her side in a second, catching her before she falls.

"Hudson..."

Before she gets a chance to say anything else, I kneel down and pick her up, hauling her over my shoulder.

"Hudson!" she protests. "What on earth are you doing? You can't just... just... kidnap me!" Her little fists rain down on my back, but she relaxes in my hold. Her body trusts me, now I just need her heart and mind to do the same.

"We weren't done with our conversation," I grunt, patting her thighs before gripping her tight. "You can cry, you can shout, you can call me every name in the book, but I'm not going to let you run away before we get a chance to work this out."

Sydney falls silent as I stride into the bar, right back to my office. I set my woman back down on the couch, then grab a water bottle from my desk, handing it to her. I let Sydney collect her thoughts while she sips on the water. I meant what I said. I'll take whatever she dishes out as long as she's mine at the end of the day.

I pace back and forth, wanting to give her time to think, but needing to burn off this energy somehow.

"I don't know what you want from me," she finally says, her voice soft and tentative as she looks down at her hands.

"I just want to talk, sweetheart. I don't understand what happened. Whenever you're ready, I need you to walk me through what you're thinking so we can work through it together." When she doesn't say anything for a moment, I fear I messed up again. I'm about to apologize when Sydney finally speaks.

"Why?"

"Why do I want to understand what happened?" Sydney nods. "Sweetheart, because I want to know how to fix it. I know your anxiety is telling you all sorts of things right now, and I want to be the person you come to for help figuring out what's real."

"But, why?"

"Why?" I repeat, dumbfounded by her question. I stop my pacing and kneel down in front of her, placing my hands on her knees. "Don't you know how much I love you? Couldn't you feel it last night? This morning?"

Her eyes go wide and her mouth drops as she gapes at me. "But... you never said anything."

"I'm not so good with words around you, remember?" I give her a little smile, relieved when she returns it.

"It's just three little ones. I think even you can handle it." Christ, when she smirks at me and her green eyes sparkle, I nearly topple over. This woman is so fucking mine.

I cup Sydney's face, stroking her cheeks with my thumbs. Her soft skin grounds me and gives me the confidence to press on. "I love you," I whisper, kissing her forehead. "I love you," I repeat, pressing my lips to her temples and cheeks. "I love you," I murmur, my lips barely brushing hers.

Sydney blinks back tears and then smiles so wide I think my heart might give out. I need to taste it on her lips.

Closing the distance between us, I capture her mouth and slide my tongue inside, claiming her and branding her with all of my love and devotion. Sydney throws her arms around my neck, clinging to me as I pull her off the couch and into my lap.

When we break apart, I tuck her hair behind her ear and kiss her forehead. "Now that we have that settled, let's talk about your job offer. Tell me what you're excited about."

She sighs, leaning her head against my shoulder. "I don't know if I'm *excited* about the receptionist job, but it's still a great opportunity."

I nod my head thoughtfully, trying to look at things from her perspective. "You said the design firm is a well-respected one. Is it a dream of yours to work there as a designer?"

She thinks about it for a moment before answering. "No, I guess not. It's not like I've been pining over one particular firm or another. It would look good on my resume though." After a beat, she continues. "It's safe. I know what's expected of me. I'll follow orders for a year or two and then work my way up."

I hum and nod my head, but I don't interject my thoughts. I want her to work through this without my demands. I need her to know I won't steamroll her or belittle her because it takes her a little more time to process things.

"But, yes, I hear what you're saying about getting experience here. And who knows what my portfolio might look like in a year if I stuck around here? I could have several projects already under my belt instead of answering phones and sucking up to the bosses."

Once again, I simply nod, combing my fingers through her hair while she takes a few deep breaths.

"I'm scared," she admits softly. I tighten my hold on her and kiss the top of her head. "I don't do well in the spotlight."

I smile and nuzzle into the side of her neck, kissing right below her ear. "Then change the lighting. I hear that helps."

Sydney giggles, the sound filling my chest as it echoes around the room. "I think you're getting better with your words. And your timing."

I chuckle, loving the spark of sassiness in her gaze. "I'm trying real damn hard here, sweetheart. I'd like the opportunity to improve every day, with you by my side." I kiss her hairline and then rest my forehead on hers. "You're calling the shots here, beautiful. You want to stay? I'll do everything in my power to get your business off the ground. You want to move to Denver? I'll be right there with you."

"Really?" she gasps.

"Of course. I told you I'm not letting you go. I'd never want to take an opportunity away from you, especially if it's building the career of your dreams. I just want to make sure you're not sacrificing your happiness for the feeling of safety. I'll be your safe place, Sydney. You can have it all if you just let me help. Let me in."

She sniffles and wipes a few tears from her eyes. My gut twists and I fear I fucked it up for a final time.

"You're right," she finally whispers. "My grandma told me to choose my future based on hope, not fear. If I went to Denver, it would be out of fear that I'll fail on my own. But when I think about staying here, when I think about... you, all I feel is hope and happiness."

"Thank fuck." I exhale forcefully and then kiss my woman with everything in me. She returns it, deepening our kiss until I'm drowning in her.

"I'm sorry I got a little crazy," she says once we run out of breath from our kiss.

"You're not crazy, sweet girl. Just promise me we'll talk things out. No more running away."

"No more running away," she agrees.

"Now, let me take my woman upstairs and give her so much pleasure she can't walk, let alone run."

Sydney's eyes grow dark, her skin heated as she blushes for me. "Those are some serious words, mister. Can you back them up?"

"Fuck yes," I growl, lifting her up into my arms.

Sydney giggles as I carry her up to my apartment, not caring about the customers staring at us. Most of them have grins on their faces, and I have no doubt Grams told them all about her plan to get us together. They are just happy to see another Connie Wolf plan come to fruition.

As soon as we're inside my bedroom, I tear my mouth away from hers just long enough to peel her dress and bra off, and then my lips are back on her skin, trailing down her neck. "Need to be inside you, love," I murmur into the shell of her ear. Sydney lets out a sexy, needy little whimper as I slip my hand into her soaking wet panties. My fingers part her folds and find her clit, massaging circles over the bundle of nerves. "Damn, you need it too, don't you?"

"God yes, Hudson. I need you. Please, please, don't make me wait." Hearing her beg for me is sweeter than anything I've ever experienced. A wave of pleasure rushes down my spine, drawing my balls up tight and making precum leak out of me like a damn faucet. Fuck, this woman is my undoing.

I rid her of the last remaining scrap of fabric, then lift her up into my arms, carrying my incredible woman to bed. I toss her on the mattress and then strip down, adrenaline pumping in my veins and urging me to claim her right the fuck now.

Sydney is spread out for me on the bed, her chocolatey hair a tangled mess, her swollen lips slightly parted, her chest heaving with shallow breaths. Goddamn, she's gorgeous. And *mine*. She's all mine.

I climb on the bed and crawl up her body, kissing her thighs, torso, breasts, neck, and finally, her sweet lips. I rub my body against hers, needing that friction, needing to feel her skin against mine, needing to prove she's really here.

"I'm right here," she whispers, cupping my cheek. I stare into her bright green eyes, not even questioning how she read my mind. She knows me, sees me, understands me in a way no one else ever has.

I nod and take a breath, centering myself once more. Sydney presses her lips to mine, her tongue seeking entrance. I give my girl everything she wants, opening my mouth to welcome her kiss.

It starts off slow, with tentative licks. Sydney explores my mouth, then pulls my bottom lip through her teeth, making me growl. She grins mischievously at me, and fuck, it physically pains me to hold back my orgasm. Shit, this can't be over before it even begins.

"You like knowing you have control over me, love?"

"Mmhm," she nods, her lip twisting into a flirty smile.

Sydney gasps and then giggles as I flip our positions so she's on top. "Then take it, beautiful. Take control."

She braces herself on my chest, pushing herself up and adjusting to our new position. For a second, Sydney looks unsure of herself, but all of that vanishes when she sees my angry cock trapped between our bodies.

Sydney grabs the fucker and squeezes. Hard. "Jesus Christ," I growl as I clench my fists.

She grins again, knowing exactly the kind of power she has over me. I slide my hands up her thighs and squeeze, helping her rock against me. Sydney licks her damn lips as she rolls her hips, rubbing her pussy up and down my shaft. The head of my cock taps her clit and she shivers, repeating the motion.

I reach out and cup her tits, weighing them in my hands and brushing my thumbs over her nipples.

"Yes," she hisses out, her movements stuttering as she leans into my touch.

I play with her hardened peaks, twisting them and plucking them while Sydney claws at my chest and rubs against me, getting herself off without me even entering her.

Sydney's movements grow frantic as she writhes on top of me. Her cream drips from her pussy, so close to coming already. A shiver runs down her spine and she holds her breath, preparing for her orgasm. I feel it pushing forward, demanding to be felt, making her whimper with each breath.

Right before it takes her under, I grip her hips and hold her still. Sydney looks down at me with confusion and frustration but then understanding dawns on her when I line myself up with her entrance. I groan when I feel her tight little channel pulse around the head of my cock. Goddamn, her greedy little pussy is trying to suck me inside.

She shocks the hell out of me by growling back and then slamming her tight as fuck pussy down on my cock.

"Jesus fuck!" I roar. I help her rock against me and circle her hips, finding what feels good.

"Yes!" Sydney cries out, wiggling her hips and hitting her G-spot against my thick dick. She shudders and moans, rolling her sexy fucking body on top of mine, totally taking control of her pleasure.

She leans back, resting her hands on my thighs and baring her beautiful body to me while she rides my cock. I slide one hand up her torso while the other squeezes her ass and opens her up even more for me.

I cup her breast and pinch her nipple, groaning when more of her cream spills out. Jesus, I barely manage to keep it together when I look down and see where we're connected. Watching her tight, wet little cunt stretch obscenely wide to take in my many inches is something I'll remember for the rest of my life.

"That's it, Sydney. That's so fucking it," I growl, moving both of my hands to her hips, jerking her up and down as I meet her thrust for thrust. Her pussy flutters around me as her muscles lock up tight.

Sydney rolls forward, resting her hands on either side of my head. Her lips find mine and we kiss and fuck like the world is burning down around us and this is our last chance to find love and passion.

She buries her face into the side of my neck and sobs as her body shakes and tightens around me. My beautiful woman bites my neck and creams all over my cock as she reaches her climax.

Feeling her orgasm absolutely devastate her snaps something inside of me.

I roll over, changing our position and fucking into that little pussy, unable to control myself. Her back bows off the bed and her legs wrap around me, holding me close. She digs her heels into my ass and claws my back, leaving her mark on me as another orgasm rattles through her.

"So good, baby," I growl, before claiming her lips as my own.

I devour her, biting at her lips and spearing my tongue inside of her eager mouth, licking up every inch and then sucking on her tongue. It's a wild, messy kiss, one that matches the way I'm fucking her like a goddamn animal.

I slide one hand down her body and grip her ass cheek, changing the angle of her hips and helping her meet me thrust for thrust. My cock scrapes against her most sensitive spot with each fierce stroke.

She's breaking apart for me; I can feel it. Every time I hit the end of her, she cracks a little more, the pressure of her orgasm building and pulsing and pushing her boundaries.

My balls draw up tight as my own orgasm gathers in the base of my spine. My rhythm falters slightly as I try to hold on, needing her to come with me. "Get there, baby, fuck, please get there. Need one more from you."

"It's too much, too much, I'm scared..."

"I've got you, Sydney. Let go for me, I'm right here. Let go, love. Come for me."

She sucks in a huge breath and holds it, her whole body trembling and then freezing. Every damn muscle is pulled so tight as she clings to me with everything she has. With one last brutal thrust, we both shatter completely.

Sydney floods my cock with her release, and I give her everything in return, my cum splashing into her throbbing pussy as she sucks down every last drop. We're both grunting, shaking, sweating as we ride that high together.

Eventually, she goes limp in my arms. I bury my face into the side of her neck and pump into her twice more before collapsing. I roll to the side and drape my freshly fucked little angel over my chest.

"Holy shit," she mumbles into my chest, her voice all scratchy as she catches her breath.

"Yeah," I agree, just as worn out and awed as she is.

Sydney lifts her head up, piercing me with those green eyes. They are glassy with tears, and while I want to haul her on top of me and kiss them away, I get the sense she needs to tell me something.

"Hudson?" she whispers.

I smile softly at her. "Yeah, sweetheart?"

"I love you too, you know."

I close my eyes, breathing in her declaration. "Again," I murmur.

"I love you."

"Fuck, again," I growl, tipping my head down to look at my beautiful woman. She leans up, her lips an inch from mine.

"I love you with all of me, Hudson Wolf. Thank you for not giving up on me."

"I could say the same to you, sweet girl. Thank you for giving me a million chances to make a good impression." Her smile lights up the whole damn world, and I know what I need to do next. I wasn't planning on it so soon, but fuck it. I'm all in. "I'm hoping to get this right the first time," I say, adjusting her so I can reach out and grab the little box on the nightstand.

"What is that?"

"Why don't you take a look?" I hand her the box and watch as she opens it. Her mouth drops and she looks from me to the antique ring and back again. It's a bit old-fashioned, with an emerald in the center of the band, flanked by smaller diamonds on either side.

This time, it's Sydney who is out of words.

"I love you, Sydney. I love everything about you, from your cute button nose to your sexy as hell curves. I love how thoughtful you are, and how you pay attention to the little details. I love the way your laughter fills up my soul. I swear, baby, your smile makes life worth living. I can't wait to be with you forever, to support you, and watch you grow more and more confident. I just need one little word from you."

Tears flow down her cheeks as she takes the ring out, examining it closely.

"It's my Grams's ring," I say, hoping it's not a deal-breaker. "But I can get you a different one. I just thought—"

"It's perfect," she whispers, slipping it on her ring finger.

"Is that a yes?"

Sydney grins and then weaves her hands in my hair pulling me down for a wild kiss.

"Yes," she breathes out, her lips finding mine once more. "Yes, yes, yes," she chants, kissing me and giggling while still holding me close.

"God, I love you so much, Sydney. I think I have from day one."

"Maybe you should have started with that then," she teases as she settles back down on my chest.

I pinch her side, making her shriek and squirm against me. "My sweet, sassy girl," I rasp against her ear. "I'll start every day like that from now on. Letting you know how much I love you and how precious you are."

"That sounds perfect," she says with a sleepy sigh, cuddling up closer to me.

"You're perfect."

"You're getting a little cheesy," she says with a grin, her eyelids fluttering closed.

I chuckle and pull the blankets over us. "I'll have to work on that."

"Mmkay..." She drifts off with a smile on her face and my ring on her finger.

This is how it was always supposed to be. I'll do everything in my power to have this every single day. To say I'll love Sydney forever doesn't even begin to cover it. I'll love her from now until infinity, and even then, it won't be long enough. I can't wait to get started.

Epilogue

Sydney

I take one last look around the living room, making sure the curtains are open just the right amount to let some soft, natural light in. All the artwork is straight and evenly spaced, and I even added a little bowl of candy to the coffee table. The bowl matches the accent pillows, of course.

"Sydney! Oh my goodness, this is *gorgeous*!"

I beam at Mrs. Traeger, my smile stretching so wide my cheeks hurt. I've worked on hundreds of rooms, businesses, and events in the six years since I started my own interior design business, but the initial reveal to the client never gets old. I absolutely love knowing I was able to take their vision and make it a reality.

"I'm so glad you think so, Mrs. Traeger. I'm glad we decided to stick with the original paint colors. I think it was the accents and lighting that really needed a touch-up."

"You're right about that, and I trust your judgment. Thank you so much for your work on my home these last few weeks. I'm absolutely in love with this space all over again."

"That's exactly why I do what I do," I tell her truthfully, unable to hide my smile.

We part ways after she writes a check for the second half of my payment. I get half up front, a lesson I learned the hard way after a difficult client screwed me over, and half when the job is complete.

I make my way home, excited to be done with another project. I always give myself a few days off in between clients to make sure I get some rest and spend quality time with my family. Hudson noticed I was getting burnt out after handling several big projects back to back, so he sat me down and we discussed a better, more sustainable schedule.

Hudson and I got married a few months after he proposed. He wanted to get married the next day down at the courthouse, but I told him I wanted to plan and design my dream wedding. He was all in, helping me with every decision and being the perfect mix of supportive and strong.

He's been so good to me these last six years. Whenever I'm feeling overwhelmed, anxious, or stressed, I know I can find him and melt into his embrace. Hudson knows when it's all too much, and he's always right there to pull me aside and give me space to breathe and talk about whatever is on my mind.

I pull into the driveway, smiling when I see Hudson crawling around on the ground with our two kids, Holly and Charles. Holly just turned three, and Charles is five. He's the best older brother to her, and I know she'll always have a protector in him.

"What's going on over here?" I ask, squatting down beside the kids. Hudson looks up at me, giving me his warmest smile. God, I'll never get over how handsome he is.

"We're following ants!" Charles exclaims, wiggling from excitement. Holly nods in agreement, pointing at the trail of ants marching in and out of a small anthill. I smile at them, loving how close they are already.

"How was work? Did Mrs. Traeger love her new living room?"

"She did," I say, unable to hide my smile.

"I knew she would. I'm so proud of you, sweetheart." He tells me that every time I finish a project, and I know he means it.

Hudson has been my biggest supporter since day one. When I finally made the choice to stay in Rosewood, he encouraged me to ask the people I had already worked with for testimonies, which I then used for my website and ads. Hudson helped me figure out all of that as well, which is good because nothing frustrates me more than dealing with computers.

It didn't take long for word of mouth to spread around the small town, and soon my calendar was booked months in advance. It was scary at first, knowing my income was dependent on me finding clients.

Hudson stayed up late with me on many occasions, talking me through my fears and insecurities while building up my confidence at the same time.

"Shall we leave the ants to work while we get some dinner?" I ask the kids. Holly jumps up right away, wrapping her arms around my legs. I lean down and pick her up, balancing my adorable little girl on my hip.

Charles pouts, but Hudson picks him up, tickling him before throwing the giggly toddler over his shoulder. "We're ready," he announces.

I smile at my family, melting into Hudson's side as he wraps his arm around my waist. Together, the four of us head inside.

"What's got you smiling so big, sweetheart?" Hudson asks as we set the kids down to go wash up for dinner.

"I love days like this," I sigh dreamily, letting him wrap his arms around me and rock me back and forth. "I made my client happy, giving me a confidence boost in my business, I came home to my beautiful children playing in the yard, and I get to see you, my sweet, sexy husband. I could have a million days like this and never get tired of it."

"Well then, that's the goal. A million perfect days."

"How about an infinite number of days?"

"Perfect," he murmurs, nuzzling into the side of my neck. "I love you forever, beautiful."

"I love you for always," I whisper back.

Moments like these, I know I made the right choice all those years ago. I took a leap of faith, and I'll never regret choosing hope over fear.

THE END

Connect with me!

Check out my website, cameronhart.net[1], for sneak previews on my latest projects.

Follow me on social media:

Facebook Page - facebook.com/cameronhartauthor
Instagram - instagram.com/cameron.hart.author
TikTok - tiktok.com/@author.cameron.hart
Goodreads - goodreads.com/16081533.Cameron_Hart
Bookbub - bookbub.com/authors/cameron-hart

---

1. https://cameronhart.net/